EDEN-BRAZIL

Rubem Fonseca, *Winning the Game and Other Stories*
Translated by Clifford E. Landers

Jorge Amado, *Sea of Death*
Translated by Gregory Rabassa

Cristovão Tezza, *The Eternal Son*
Translated by Alison Entrekin

J.P. Cuenca, *The Only Happy Ending for a Love Story Is an Accident*
Translated by Elizabeth Lowe

Rubem Fonseca, *Crimes of August*
Translated by Clifford E. Landers

Luiz Ruffato, *Unremembering Me*
Translated by Marguerite Itamar Harrison

Moacyr Scliar, *Eden-Brazil*
Translated by Malcolm K. McNee

EDEN-BRAZIL

MOACYR SCLIAR

TRANSLATED BY MALCOLM K. MCNEE

TAGUS PRESS
UMass Dartmouth
Dartmouth, Massachusetts

*Tagus Press is the publishing arm of the
Center for Portuguese Studies and Culture at
the University of Massachusetts Dartmouth.*
Center Director: Victor K. Mendes

Brazilian Literature in Translation Series 7
Tagus Press at UMass Dartmouth
www.umassd.edu/portuguese-studies-center/
original Portuguese text © 2002 by Moacyr Scliar;
translation and translator's note © 2019 Malcolm K. McNee
Published by arrangement with Literarische Agentur Mertin Ihn. Nicole Witt
e K., Frankfurt am Main, Germany.

Manufactured in the United States of America
Executive Editor: Mario Pereira
Series Editors: Dário Borim & Cristina Mehrtens
Copyedited by Sharon Brinkman
Designed and typeset by Jen Jackowitz
Printed by Integrated Books International, Inc.

For all inquiries, please contact:
Tagus Press • Center for Portuguese Studies and Culture
UMass Dartmouth • 285 Old Westport Road
North Dartmouth, MA 02747-2300
Tel. 508-999-8255 • Fax 508-999-9272
www.umassd.edu/portuguese-studies-center/

ISBN:978- 1-933227-84-9
Library of Congress Control Number: 2019946668

CONTENTS

EDEN-
BRAZIL

1

INTRODUCING MY FRIEND, ADAMASTOR

A trip to the coast of Santa Catarina changed my life, Adamastor used to say (including in front of the TV cameras). He wasn't exaggerating. That trip really had changed his life. It changed my life too.

When I first met him, he was about forty years old. Unremarkable in appearance: neither tall nor short, neither thin nor fat. The only thing about him that drew attention, besides a somewhat bizarre goatee, was his hair, already thinning and gray, tied back in a ponytail. To the know-it-all kid that I was at the time, it seemed the trademark sign of an old geezer trying to be cool, and it contrasted with his innocent, somewhat childish looking face, reinforced by his big, light-colored eyes. That's what I said to him once: you have an innocent face, Adamastor. I didn't tell him that he had the face of a fool, or an idiot, or a dupe, or a moron; no, I just mentioned innocence, which, for me, wasn't even a defect; it could even be a quality, or at least a mark of distinction in a world in which taking advantage of others is almost the norm. But he didn't like it. He didn't appreciate being characterized as

1

innocent. He didn't say so, of course, because he was anything but confrontational, but disagreement was clearly evident in his sunburned and slightly wrinkled face.

Adamastor was the third child of a nearly bankrupt rancher from Rio Grande do Sul. Nearly bankrupt, but still authoritarian: he commanded over his family like a feudal lord. He gave no consideration to his children; he ignored them, preferring to spend his days with his thoroughbred horses, the few that had remained of a once large herd. Adamastor never got along with his father; his mother, a gentle, though melancholy, woman, tried to bridge the distance between them, but with no success. The fact is that Adamastor hated life on the ranch, and as soon as he could he followed the example of his brothers, leaving to go study in the state capital. Obeying a single imposition of his father, he applied for an undergraduate program in agronomy. He had no interest in this profession, which his father deemed important ("The future of the countryside is in science and technology"), but, during his course of studies, he had two significant experiences. The first, political, was born of his friendship with Marcelo, a classmate. Like Adamastor, Marcelo had never felt particularly attracted to agronomy; but he had decided to enroll in that program anyway. Not due to pressure from his father, also a big rancher, quite successful, and who had granted his son the freedom to choose any major or even skip college altogether. The concession of a large landholder with aristocratic pretensions, Marcelo used to say. He had decided on agronomy for another reason. The real problem in this country is the unequal distribution of land, he used to say, and the path to revolution passes through the fight for land reform.

He wanted to take part in that fight, but not simply as a politician. As a technician too. It's not good enough to simply give speeches to the peasants, he would say, we need to teach them how to plant. He dismissed the theorists who spoke of the struggle for land reform but had never harvested a single ear of corn. The fact is, however, that he didn't go to class. He spent his time in meetings, and at night he would go out to spray-paint the walls with slogans—he didn't have time for his studies. He failed all of his classes, and he ended up dropping out of the university. Without his friend's influence, Adamastor, who had never been a leftist of much conviction—the books that Marcelo had loaned him piled up on his nightstand, unread—little by little abandoned revolutionary ideas. In part because, in the meantime, he discovered within himself a surprising passion for environmentalism. Suddenly, he became aware of the degradation of the environment, the polluting of the air and of the rivers, the destruction of the forests. He read everything within reach, he took classes, he participated in discussion groups. He joined the environmental movement, at that time still nascent: it was during the military dictatorship, and fighting for the preservation of the environment was a form of political protest. Alongside his comrades, he participated in campaigns, he distributed flyers in the streets. That was how he met Elisa, also an activist. She wasn't very pretty or very smart, but Adamastor felt irredeemably attracted to her.

This passion was not entirely reciprocated. Elisa was a difficult girl; she found it much easier to shout slogans in the streets than make love. Even so, and with the help of friends, their courtship eventually led to marriage—lukewarm at first and then full of resentment. They had no support from Adamastor's father, who didn't even go to the wedding reception—he couldn't stand his daughter-in-law, whom he considered half crazy. Adamastor was still a student, so, in order to support themselves, Elisa had to abandon her degree in social sciences and work in an office—which made her even more insufferable. Fights were frequent; the two of them reached a point where they could barely tolerate each other. The birth of a son improved the situation a bit, but soon they were at each other's throats again: they argued about who should get up in the middle of the night to change the baby's diapers, who should take him to daycare. The boy became increasingly anxious and irritable, crying over any small thing.

The couple's relationship became even more strained due to Adamastor's mediocrity in his profession. After graduating, he refused to take over administration of the family property, which infuriated his father. Adamastor could thus no longer count on any form of support. The solution was to find a job in the government, and that's what Adamastor did, securing a position in a federal agricultural agency. It had something to do with environmental protection, which in theory interested him, but the work was purely bureaucratic; he spent the day reviewing and submitting reports, which gave him not the least bit of satisfaction. Marcelo, who phoned him once in a while, used to say, in a spiteful tone, you're paying the price for your accommodation to bourgeois principles.

As if this weren't enough, there was a practical problem. A serious practical problem. Adamastor didn't earn much. He could barely pay his rent and meet basic household expenses. They needed to spend less, something Elisa would not accept. Tired of poverty, as she herself used to say, she demanded a lifestyle entirely incompatible with her husband's salary. The son, Herodotus, took sides with his mother. He had his own demands. The most important: he wanted to go to Disney World at least once a year, like his cousins, the children of one of Elisa's brothers, a successful architect.

Adamastor ended up asking for a divorce. He got it, but not even then did he have any peace. His ex-wife called him every day, to complain that he was late with the alimony and child support and to insult him: you're nothing but a failure, a big loser. In short, a tormented existence.

2

ADAMASTOR'S PROJECT

And so, the big turnaround: an old bachelor uncle, whom Adamastor had regularly visited, died and, to his surprise, left him a nice inheritance. Once in possession of the money, Adamastor decided to teach his ex-wife a lesson: he bought her a brand-new, spectacular apartment, a car, and—for the first time—he took his son to Disney World. Finally, grumbled Herodotus, when his father announced what he thought would be great news. They embarked on their trip, just the two of them: Elisa, celebrating the unexpected affluence, had invited a friend of hers to take a trip to Europe. Adamastor, who missed his son a great deal, hoped that the trip would be the much longed-for opportunity to bond again. After all, they would be together for ten days; they could talk, learn about each other again.

The trip, however, was a disaster. The boy wasn't at all interested in Disney World's attractions. He just wanted to buy stuff— videogames, mainly—and complain: this hotel's a dump, the waiters aren't serving us properly, you could have come up with something better.

"After all, you're rich, aren't you?" was the constant and sarcastic question.

Adamastor returned home so tired and irritated that he decided to repay himself with another trip. His destination, this time, would be quite different: a nearly unknown beach in Santa Catarina. There, when he was nineteen, he had spent the happiest summer of his life, camping with a few friends (and girlfriends, of course). During the day, they would go for hikes, play soccer, swim in the ocean; at night they would have bonfires and drink and sing into the wee hours. He now went off in search of those memories, driving his imported car. But his memory failed him; he could no longer quite remember the beach's exact location, and he ended up getting lost, which ended up being a true twist of fate. Following a poorly maintained dirt road, Adamastor arrived at the top of a hill, from which there was an absolutely stunning view: a completely deserted beach ringed by mountains and backed by a large expanse of native forest. Adamastor, stunned, stopped the car and got out. It was all so beautiful, so peaceful—so pure—that he began to sob. This surprised him; he hadn't cried for a very long time. Not even his father's death had really moved him. The tears were, then, proof of something transcendent. He had found, finally, his life's purpose: he wanted to live on that beach, make his home there. And not just that. He was certain that it was the ideal place for the realization of a project that for a long time had been taking shape in his head.

An environmental project. The remains of his activist past? Perhaps. Like many urban Brazilians, Adamastor was convinced that a good deal of his unhappiness could be attributed to the dehumanized megalopolis where he lived, a city of giant, ugly buildings, of clogged streets and avenues; a violent, aggressive place. But he went even further. He wanted to make this dissatisfaction the point of departure for a project. A place that would provide people with a refuge, even if temporary, from a stressful, meaningless life.

What he had in mind, in short, was a theme park.

Disney World? No way. Adamastor had hated that massive, artificial thing. His park would be the exact opposite. To begin with, he would highlight what was greatest and most original about Brazil: nature, in all of its pungent glory. Flora and fauna would be the main attractions. Instead of Donald Duck, the picturesque *ema*; instead of Mickey, the armadillo. The capybara. The *paca*. The comical *sagüi*. And the trees, the plants, all carefully preserved, all presented to the visitors by trained guides. People would spend days there, watching birds, studying flowers. No, not studying: communicating with them. What can you tell me of life, camellia? Hmm, camellia, what do you say? You say I should live life differently, camellia? How about that, camellia? You read my mind, camellia. You are more than just a flower, camellia, you are a teacher. Quiet, patient, reserved, but infinitely wise. Oh, you don't agree, petunia? Why don't you find your colleague, camellia, wise? Oh, you don't want to say? To be frank, petunia, it sounds like envy to me, you hear, you rascal? Yes, envy. Floral envy, but envy all the same. I know that you flowers have feelings. A lot of people recognize this, but the common understanding is that it only includes nice feelings, lyrical stuff. It doesn't occur to anyone that a petunia could be envious. However, don't think that this disappoints me, petunia, or frustrates me. To the contrary, I'm happy to know that I can discover in you, beautiful flower, a bit of envy. This means that I'm in perfect harmony with you, flowers. This means that my empathy with you is complete. Thank you, camellia. Thank you, petunia.

Dialogue with the flowers: one activity. But not the only one. The theme park's schedule of events would be intense: tours, classes, workshops. And work too. For example, the visitors would prepare their own meals, with exclusively natural foods—no additives, no artificial ingredients, all authentic, just as life should be authentic. At the theme park, people would rediscover the meaning of existence.

This, we should briefly note, was not Adamastor's first project. During prior moments of daydreaming, he had thought of eco-design houses, natural cooking classes, a whale refuge. None of these projects moved forward—for lack of money, but mainly for lack of sustained enthusiasm. Adamastor was a chronic depressive, for which his wife constantly criticized him, irritated by his lack of initiative and energy. Energy, now, would not be found lacking, of this he was certain. Nor—of fundamental importance—would money.

On that very day, Adamastor set himself to the task. First, he tried to find out who owned the land. He went to the closest small town; there they told him that there was one guy who knew everything about the region: the barber.

He sat in the chair in the tiny barbershop, and, while the man trimmed his goatee, he asked his question.

"The land belongs to a widow, *Senhora* Cota," said the barber. "Since you're asking, are you interested in buying it?"

"Maybe," Adamastor cautiously responded. "Why?"

The barber smiled, a malicious, knowing smile.

"Because she's a complicated woman. Sometimes she wants to sell everything, even puts an ad in the paper—but when it comes time to close the deal she backs out. She's very attached to that house. She lived there with her husband, her children were born there. So you're going to have to be very clever."

Adamastor thanked him for the information and went to find *Senhora* Cota. Getting there wasn't easy; in fact, the property stretched along the edges of two steep hills, one at either end of the beautiful bay that had left him so ecstatic. *Senhora* Cota's house, which was very large and built in the colonial style, was at the top of one of the hills. It was possible to get close by car, but from there you had to go by foot, down a trail. Another trail descended to the beach, passing through a clearing in the middle of the jungle.

Adamastor rang the bell at the entrance. Nothing, no answer. He rang again, and then again. Finally, the door opened, and there appeared a tiny old woman with a shriveled face and a look of suspicion. She didn't invite him in. To the contrary.

"What do you want?" she asked brusquely, and she then added: "I'll tell you straight away, if you're selling something, you've knocked on the wrong door. I don't have any money to spend, and even if I did I wouldn't give it to a traveling salesman. You're nothing more than a band of thieves and con men."

Surprised by her aggressiveness and, frankly, intimidated, Adamastor said that he wasn't there to sell anything, to the contrary.

"I've come to make you an offer, *Senhora* Cota."

"Ah, so you know my name . . . I see you've been going around gathering information about me. What kind of an offer?"

"An offer for your land."

She wrinkled her brow.

"An offer for my land? Ah, yes, now I see. You're not a salesman. You must be a real estate agent. Am I right?"

Adamastor tried to smile but couldn't. His embarrassment—no, his unease—was increasing.

"No, ma'am. I'm not a real estate agent. But I do want to buy your property."

She laughed, sarcastically.

"You're not the first, and you won't be the last. Every so often people come by with these sorts of proposals. Nobody's convinced me."

"But my case is different," said Adamastor, already desperate. He noticed that he was sweating a great deal, and it wasn't just due to the heat. He wiped his forehead with a handkerchief and continued: "You see, I have a proposal for this area."

He smiled, forcibly (determinedly, like a spokesperson, it was a disaster).

"A wonderful project, I guarantee it."

She looked him over, skeptically.

"Oh yeah? So tell me about this project."

Adamastor took a deep breath and began to reveal what he had in mind. A difficult task. The woman could barely hear, and she constantly interrupted him, asking him to speak up.

"You look like you're dying, I've never seen somebody speak so quietly. What's the matter? Did the climb up here wear you out?"

Adamastor was flustered; he stuttered things about the quality of life of modern man, about changes in lifestyle. He felt like he wasn't explaining it right. In fact, after a bit, the woman interrupted him.

"Now I understand what your deal is. You must be the leader of some sort of sect, one of those churches that keep popping up all over the place. All this talk about a new life doesn't fool me. You want to settle in here, erect some sort of temple, attract the naïve with promises of miracles and who knows what else. Fine, if that's what you want, then you've knocked on the wrong door, my friend. I'm not one to be taken advantage of."

This was just too much. Adamastor protested, weakly. No, it's not at all what you're thinking, he was going to say, but he couldn't, he simply wasn't able to finish the sentence. Resting himself against the doorframe, he started to cry, convulsively.

(As he himself later said, it wasn't simply because of that unpleasant conversation that he was crying. It was because of everything: because of his unhappy childhood, because of the troubled relationship with his father, because of his failed marriage, because of his mediocre career. And it was because of his incredible incapacity for dealing with stuff in life, an incapacity that even prevented him from saying to someone what he intended to say. His father, his wife, the boss at the office, they were all right: he was a disaster.)

The woman looked at him in silence. Shocked at first, and then moved—deep down she must have been a good person—she invited him into the house, had him sit down, and brought him a glass of water. When Adamastor finally had calmed down, she asked him to tell her again about the project.

"But now explain it to me properly, so I can understand."

Her hand cupped to her ear, she listened attentively. Adamastor, at her side, was now inspired: he eloquently described the merits of a theme park centered on nature in a country in which the environment was being unmercifully, criminally destroyed.

A pause. A few minutes went by—minutes that, to Adamastor, seemed an eternity—and then the old woman revealed her toothless gums in a smile.

"You are the person I've been waiting for all these years," she said. "The person to whom I can entrust my land, the only thing I have left. I'm sure you're a good, honest man, and that you will take care of all this just as my husband and I took care of it for so many years. Make your offer, and if it's what I expect is fair, the land is yours."

3

EDEN-BRAZIL IS BORN

In less than a week, the transaction was concluded. The old woman, *Senhora* Cota, was helpful with the final details, explaining to him everything that he needed to know about the property and even showing him places where the Indians had left behind curious inscriptions—which Adamastor could show to visitors. And, wishing him happiness, she said goodbye; she would go to São Paulo, where a daughter lived. Adamastor moved into the house, which *Senhora* Cota had left furnished, with the electricity and telephone still connected. He would live there, and there he would set up, provisionally, the general headquarters of the project. For which he felt entirely mobilized: it wasn't a business endeavor, it was a cause—a cause that would provide meaning for his previously empty existence, the cause that would represent his mark upon the world.

He began by making a list of all the tasks he would need to accomplish. They were many. To begin with, he would have to undertake a detailed study of the flora and fauna of the region.

After all, these were the basis for the sort of ecotourism he intended.

Despite his degree in agronomy, he did not have sufficient knowledge to do this himself. He needed help. He telephoned an old professor of his who was also connected to the environmental movement.

"You're going to need specialists," the man said.

He recommended a botanist and a zoologist. Adamastor hired the two of them, set them up in the house, and asked that they do the work as quickly as possible. Both of them immediately got started. Two weeks later, they brought him their findings.

"There's good news and bad news," said the botanist, a young man, recently graduated, with a comical expression on his face.

The good news: from an ecological point of view, the region was very well preserved—precisely because the woman didn't permit access to anyone and hadn't undertaken any "improvements."

"Great," said Adamastor. "And the bad news?"

"I don't think your park has much to show. The flora and fauna are well preserved, but there isn't anything really interesting. Especially as far as tourists are concerned. Those people want spectacular things. Waterfalls. Elephants. Giraffes. Carnivorous plants. You know, the stuff they show on safaris, for example. And you don't have anything like that."

He paused, and then added, "It's not my business, and you didn't ask for advice, but if I were you I would give up on the idea. Or, if not, I would provide some extra attractions."

That was exactly what Adamastor didn't want to hear. "Attractions" brought to mind a resort, a theme park, Disney World. Attractions: snack bar, souvenir shop, an auditorium for shows by country music duos. That is, mediocrity. Or, fakeness. As soon as he started adding attractions, whatever they might be, the project would no longer be what it was that he had in mind, it would be another sideshow, like so many others throughout Brazil.

On the other hand, however, Adamastor wanted visitors. Wasn't that his goal, to change people? In order to change people, after all, he needed them to come to see his project. Now he didn't want cheap thrills. He wanted something different, a special attraction—something authentic. It's just that nothing came to mind, and that's what he said to the zoologist. The man thought about it a bit.

"There is somebody who can solve your problem, and who, as a matter of fact, lives not too far from here."

"Who?"

"Ernesto Gutiérrez."

Adamastor didn't recognize the name. The zoologist explained: he was an Argentine who had come to the region a number of years ago, hired to run a luxury hotel—a large development that was to be financed by European businessmen. The financing never came through, and the hotel never got any further than the blueprints. Gutiérrez, however, had decided to stick around: he liked the beach, which was something Buenos Aires didn't have to offer. Single, he lived alone, though female company was never in short supply. Once in a while he would travel for some consulting work, but he always returned to his beach and his boat, the *Cambalache*.

Adamastor decided to find him. He dialed the number that the zoologist had given him. Gutiérrez himself answered and was effusive.

"Come on over and have a whisky with me, and we'll talk about your project."

Adamastor got in his car and drove there. It was a large, Mediterranean-style beach house, a bit gaudy. A servant greeted him and led him to the veranda, where there was a stunning view of the sea. Gutiérrez was there: a middle-aged, sunburnt man with gray hair carefully combed back, and a trimmed mustache. He was dressed head to toe in an immaculate white: shirt, shorts, socks, tennis shoes. Adamastor had expected to find some tango dancer type, but, to his relief, Gutiérrez looked more like a dynamic business executive, though one on vacation. Charming, friendly, well spoken, he enthusiastically welcomed his visitor, inviting him to have a seat, and offering him a drink (Adamastor refused the drink: he wanted to make it perfectly clear that the issue at hand was serious, and he didn't normally drink anyway) and then also sat down.

"Okay. I'm all ears."

They talked for a long time. Gutiérrez asked a number of questions. Adamastor responded, but a bit insecurely. Interrogated, he became aware of the fact that even in his own mind the project wasn't really well defined: there were gaps, unresolved issues. To an outsider, and especially to someone as astute and clever as Gutiérrez, it must have seemed half fantasy. Or complete fantasy. He decided to confess.

"You must be thinking that I don't have the thing completely formulated . . ."

"That's exactly what I'm thinking: you don't have the thing completely formulated." He laughed: "Like they say around here, you've heard the rooster crow, but you don't know where."

He took a swallow of his drink, remained silent for a moment, staring off into the distance. Then he looked at Adamastor.

"But there is no doubt that it's a wonderful idea. Very original, with good potential. It won't be hard to turn it into a solid, profitable venture."

"And can you do that?" Adamastor asked, barely containing his excitement.

Gutiérrez laughed, immodestly.

"Can I do that? My friend, if I'm unable to solve your problem, I'll go back to Argentina."

A pause, and then he added.

"Of course it will cost you some money. My fees, to begin with."

He mentioned a far from modest sum. Adamastor, however, didn't protest; he was sure that Gutiérrez was the right man to advise him. If it cost some money, have patience. It wasn't the right time to worry about expenses.

"Very good. And when can you start?"

Gutiérrez asked for a week to study the idea and to detail his suggestions. And, in fact, exactly seven days later he came calling, carrying an impressively thick folder: the project.

It wasn't exactly what Adamastor was hoping for. Sure, it included excursions along nature trails and also the stuff with animals and plants; but on this point, the primary one as far as Adamastor was concerned, only five summary lines were dedicated. The bulk of the document contemplated a project that, while taking into consideration environmental conditions, still was grandiose in nature. It proposed a hotel, for example. Small, it would run on solar energy, as would be expected of a place concerned with nature conservation—but it was a hotel of some considerable luxury. It would include a small shopping center. Sure, it would sell natural products—but still, it was a shopping center. The restaurant would have a vegetarian selection, but it would mainly serve international cuisine. The spa would offer mud baths—but alongside it there would be a modern fitness center. That is, ecology plus consumerism. Ecology plus profit.

"All this will need to be marketed well," Gutiérrez concluded. "You know, without a bit of advertising and promotion, nothing works. We'll have to immediately hire a publicist and a spokesperson. I can refer you to some I know that are competent and trustworthy."

Adamastor listened in silence. The plans were impressive; but was this what he wanted? Was this how his dream would be materialized? He had some doubts, which Gutiérrez, clever as he was, did not fail to notice.

"You don't seem very satisfied with the plan. So let's have it, tell me what's bothering you."

Adamastor hesitated for an instant, but—after all, it was his land, his money—he let loose: the project was quite ambitious, and it could truly be something new in terms of tourism, but it wasn't really what he had in mind.

"Hotel, fitness center . . . Frankly, that's not what I wanted. Excuse me for saying, but I have to be honest with you."

He stood up, looked out for some time at the landscape, and, finally, he turned back to face the Argentine.

"You see, Gutiérrez, this here is like paradise. I don't want to transform it into just another tourist attraction. It would be a crime against nature. Like so many other crimes committed in this country. Right here, for example, on the coast . . ."

He talked and he talked. Gutiérrez looked as if he wasn't paying attention. Suddenly he leapt from his chair.

"Like paradise! Did you say like paradise?"

Adamastor looked at him, surprised. What was so important about that phrase?

"That's what I said. Why?"

Gutiérrez didn't respond immediately. He stared off into the distance, a rapturous expression on his face. He turned back to Adamastor.

"You just gave me a great idea, Adamastor. A truly great idea. An ingenious idea, Adamastor. Ingenious. Like paradise! Simply ingenious."

Adamastor didn't understand what he was getting at. Gutiérrez laughed and hugged him.

"You don't see, Adamastor? Like paradise. Paradise! Everyone's dream! That will be the key to our project: Paradise within everyone's reach!"

Still stunned, Adamastor observed that claiming some place was like paradise didn't seem to be anything really original: he had already seen at least a dozen ads with that idea. Gutiérrez laughed.

"We aren't going to advertise paradise, Adamastor. We are going to offer Paradise, with a capital P. You know what we're going to do? We are going to reconstitute here, on the Santa Catarina coast, the Garden of Eden. We're going to keep everything that you said, eco-excursions, natural food. But we're going to offer something extra. And this something extra will make all the difference. This something extra will make the project original."

"And what is this something extra?"

Gutiérrez looked at him, and he appeared to be truly moved.

"A show. A theatrical production. I'm sure you've heard that in the Northeast they put on a Passion play that attracts thousands of tourists. We're going to do something like that. Not the Passion, of course. Our theme will be Paradise: we're going to show how Adam and Eve lived. Something completely original, Adamastor. You know how in these types of parks the guides explain to visitors what they're going to see—it's so boring and mediocre. Us, no. What we're going to offer is something surprising, unprecedented."

Adamastor wasn't getting it.

"But how are we going to do that? Don't tell me you want to build a theater here in the middle of the jungle . . ."

"Of course not. Theater? No way. We're not going to put on

a play. We're going to present a multimedia exhibit. You already said you don't want anything that looks like Disney World. No, Adamastor. Our production will take place right in the jungle. It will be like this: people arrive, they are accommodated in the hotel, and then they will be taken on an eco-tour in the jungle. There they are walking along when suddenly, boom, they come across Adam and Eve in Paradise. We're going to show all that stuff from the Bible, sin, the expulsion; but we'll make clear the idea that Paradise exists, it's intact—in my friend Adamastor's theme park. What do you think? Not even God could come up with a better promotional idea, I guarantee you."

Though still skeptical, Adamastor began to find the idea interesting. After all, as Gutiérrez said (and as the zoologist had already suggested), they needed something different, a brand: Eden, as a production, might fill the need. Of course it diverged from the original idea, but all ideas, even the most original, end up undergoing changes. So, although hesitant he ended up agreeing to the proposal.

"We can try. If it works, we'll move forward. If not, then we'll reassess."

Gutiérrez said that they would have to perfect the idea, naturally. A production like that would require careful preparation.

"Nothing amateur, Adamastor. Nothing amateur."

First of all, they would need a carefully crafted script. And they would use professional actors, a professional director, lighting and sound effects—all the elements of a great show.

"Like Broadway, Adamastor."

He caught his blunder and corrected himself.

"That is, from the technical point of view. Sure, we're not talking about a variety show, we're dealing with something serious. From this point forward, we'll have to work, and work hard."

He winked and added, "Slacking off, only in Paradise—and Paradise doesn't exist anymore." He laughed. "Doesn't exist, for now; soon we'll fill that gap, Adamastor. And now, in all seriousness . . ."

In all seriousness, they would need to get to it, the two of them, and seek out the means by which to make the plan viable. From the outset, they would have to be able to count on a small but functional base of operations. Gutiérrez already had a timeline of the various stages, and also an organizational flowchart: the general manager (Adamastor) would be in charge of three areas: hotel, mini shopping center, and spa, each with its own manager. Alongside these areas, Gutiérrez added a fourth, named by him, and not without some good-natured irony, Paradise. For which, if Adamastor agreed, he, Gutiérrez, would be directly responsible.

"I always had a thing for the theater," he revealed with pride, genuinely moved. "In Buenos Aires, I even produced three plays. One was even a success, but truth is I had to make a living and had to change professions. I never imagined I would have anything more to do with the stage, and I was resigned to that, but today, and thanks to you, Adamastor, I've rediscovered my destiny."

He put the papers back into the folder and was getting up to leave when he remembered,

"Oh, I have a name for the project."

A suspenseful pause, and then he announced, "Eden-Brazil. What do you think?"

Eden-Brazil. It was a name that never would have occurred to Adamastor, who remained silent, thinking it over.

"Eden-Brazil," Gutiérrez repeated. "Eden-Brazil! Suggestive. It evokes Paradise but also this country. The country that embraced me, Adamastor. When I was most in need."

He could not contain himself; he began to cry. Adamastor

looked at him, not knowing what to do. Finally he overcame his unease and hugged him.

"You're a great guy, Gutiérrez. And you've come up with a great name for the project."

Gutiérrez looked at him, his eyes still wet with tears.

"Thank you, Adamastor. I know Eden-Brazil is important to you. It's important to me too, believe me. I feel like this will be my life's great undertaking."

Despite their enthusiasm, complications soon began to pop up—and these had to do precisely with the image of Paradise Gutiérrez wanted to create. It's just that there was a great deal of distance between the image and the present reality. For example, the biblical Eden was home to a great variety of animal and plant species—which, Adamastor had already learned, was not the case with his property. They discussed the problem at great length. Gutiérrez suggested that they bring in animals from other parts of the country, monkeys, parrots, capybaras, agoutis.

Adamastor didn't much like the idea. Importing animals from far away had nothing to do with his understanding of ecology or his idea for a theme park. He was frank.

"Listen, Gutiérrez, I don't want to turn this place into a private zoo . . ."

The Argentine laughed.

"Who said anything about that? Not me, Adamastor, not me. Because I'm also against zoos—cages, pits, those things. All that is moronic. No, what I'm thinking is that we bring in some examples of Brazilian fauna—that can be kept free. For the kids it would be great."

Adamastor ended up agreeing. But he didn't foresee the mess he was getting himself into. In the first place, they would have to deal with animal exporters, shadowy people, not always well regarded by the Federal Environmental Protection Agency or law enforcement officials. They were told to contact a man who was known only by a nickname, Guariba, and who made a thousand demands before agreeing to speak with them: the meeting would have to take place at a certain bar in Florianópolis, at midnight on the following Monday. Adamastor and Gutiérrez went together. The bar was on the outskirts of town, a tiny place, dirty and poorly lit: a scene for a gangster movie, said Adamastor. But Guariba was there, wearing—as had been previously agreed upon—a cowboy hat and smoking a huge cigar. He invited them to sit down and slowly looked them over.

"So, you guys are interested in some critters. You know exactly what you want?"

Neither Gutiérrez nor Adamastor had an answer. With a sigh, the man opened a briefcase and took out a sort of catalogue. He opened it; it contained photographs of animals along with short descriptions of them.

"This here is an anteater. It's a toothless mammal that feeds on insects. I can offer two varieties, the collared anteater, relatively small, and the giant anteater, a marvelous creature, nearly two meters in length, a third of which is made up of its tail. This picture here is of Tamã, a completely tame anteater that likes people; you just have to whistle and he'll start wagging his tail. Here we have monkeys. People like them a lot, because of that stuff about evolution. Seems we're cousins. We have some really interesting varieties: the white-headed capuchin, the *paraguaçu* monkey, this one here—it looks like it's wearing a wig, doesn't it? And there's the night monkey, which would come in handy if you wanted to organize nighttime excursions . . . It's also known by the name *miriquiná*. This is the spider monkey, this is the brown titi, this here is known as the *macaco-inglês*—because of its face, that turns red when it gets angry—it always comes in handy for making fun of Americans . . . This is the broad-snouted caiman . . . Quite rare, very impressive, but very expensive . . . And we have birds. This here is the solitary tinamou, of the *tinamidae* family . . . The female, when it's laying its eggs, lets out a tremulous peep, crying out in agony . . . I confess that I can't hear it without weeping . . ."

Gutiérrez and Adamastor looked at the pictures, their brows creased, perplexed: brown titis, tinamous, things they'd never heard of before. Guariba understood.

"I see you two gentlemen aren't really prepared to choose. So, if it's okay with you, I can suggest some examples of exotic fauna. It all depends on how much you want to spend, my friends."

Adamastor mentioned a sum, the man pulled out a calculator and punched in a few numbers. He looked at the total and concluded, a bit irritated.

"Well, that won't get you a whole lot. About fifteen animals, maybe . . . Let's see what we can do. At any rate, the tourists are going to like them. They always like them."

He demanded half of the amount up front and told them that in ten days, at most, a truck would deliver the animals they ordered directly to Adamastor's property. He said goodbye.

"I don't need to tell you two that this transaction must remain a secret. If any information gets out, you two will be the ones paying the consequences."

Despite the threats, Guariba was a man of his word: eight days later a truck arrived at Adamastor's house hauling cages with the animals they had ordered. Adamastor demanded that they be released immediately into the jungle. A disaster: the animals either fled (a famished coati invaded a minimart along the road and was killed with a stick by the outraged shopkeeper), or they became sick, or they were stolen. In a few days, all that remained was a monkey, of some little-known species. It was an old and sickly animal; one of its eyes was covered with a cloudy film, a sort of cataract. Maybe because of this it didn't stray too far from the house, where it had a dependable source of food. Adamastor ended up growing fond of him and decided that he himself would take care of the animal, who responded to the name Lucifer.

The rest of the project also failed to develop at the expected pace. The hotel wasn't going to be very large, but even so the construction was significantly delayed, which increased Adamastor's anxiety; and the costs continued to grow. He insisted to Gutiérrez that they needed to open Eden-Brazil soon: he hoped to be able to offset the losses a bit by anticipating the income visitors would provide. The Argentine preferred to wait; he wanted a grand opening in the best of style, with everything up and running. But Adamastor insisted so much that he ended up agreeing: they would open to the public, without festivities, the part of the hotel that was finished, and it began to operate precariously. The result could not have been more disappointing. Just a few tourists showed up, and they didn't stay more than a few days.

"The place is really beautiful," one of them said. "But it's isolated, and there's nothing for us to do, no entertainment."

At that point, the show seemed to be the only hope for the project's salvation. Previously hesitant, Adamastor insisted: let's get started on it immediately. Gutiérrez, however, had not arranged for a director, or for the actors; he claimed not to know the theater scene in Brazil very well.

"We'll have to do some research, talk with people, interview candidates—and I don't have much time for all this."

Adamastor offered his assistance. "Great," said Gutiérrez, who thus saw himself relieved a bit from the constant pressure.

"If you hear of anyone, let me know."

4

INTRODUCING AN AMBITIOUS
YOUNG ACTOR: MYSELF

This was when I made my entrance in the story. And I made my entrance during a particularly tempestuous period of my life.

That year I had decided to abandon my studies in psychology at the university, which I had just begun, to become an actor instead. A difficult decision, mostly because of my family. I was the youngest child, and all the hopes of my mother, whose life had not exactly been a bed of roses, were centered on me. The daughter of immigrants in the countryside of Rio Grande do Sul, she had thought of becoming a nun. But, as in the case of Adamastor, a trip had changed her life.

When she was finishing high school, she took part in a community service program, and together with three other classmates she received a prize for her dedication from the corporate sponsor: a trip to Manaus, where, and not by chance, the corporation had a branch office.

The four young women—my mom was eighteen at the time—were lodged in a small hotel in the Amazonian capital's downtown district. Every day they would go out sightseeing or

shopping in the duty-free zone. Mom, however, wasn't interested in all that. She was, in fact, interested in a young, taciturn
Amazonian who, at a little stand set up right across from the
hotel, sold wicker and ceramic handicrafts that he himself made.
She bought a few pieces, and they started up a conversation. She
discovered that the boy's name was Peri, like the hero of José de
Alencar's romantic novel—a name that had been given to him
by a priest who was an admirer of Brazilian literature. And she
learned that he was the descendent of Indians from a now extinct
tribe. Making crafts is a way of keeping alive the traditions of my
people, he explained with a sad smile. He was sad, my father, and
always was. I think that the sadness was what most attracted my
mother. Soon they started up a romance, that clumsy, beginners'
sort of romance. Mom's friends covered for them. They snuck
my father into the hotel. Once—he was a pretty small guy—he
was brought in inside a basket, and not a very big one at that. But
her friends were apprehensive about the affair. This isn't going to
work, they warned. Mom, truly in love, paid them no heed.

The time for goodbyes arrived. It might have been the end of
the romance. It wasn't. Having promised that he would go south
after my mother, Peri was true to his word. He sold nearly everything he owned, bought a ticket, and, six months later, he showed
up in town. It was a dramatic reunion. Mom was having dinner
with the rest of the family when someone knocked at the door.
They opened it, and it was him, the *Amazonense* boy. Mom fell
into his arms, crying, everyone else staring, confused. When they
realized what was going on, mom's brothers—who considered
themselves responsible for her; they had lost their father—were
enraged. We don't want anything to do with this savage, they
shouted, even right in front of Peri. The oldest brother, Clodo-
baldo, known as Baldo, was particularly furious: the only thing
worse than an Indian is a Black, he kept repeating.

Mom stood up to them, courageously. She found a place for her boyfriend to stay, in her former teacher's house, an old communist activist who gave mom her complete support and made a point of publicly meeting with her. Soon the dispute spread throughout town and divided it, with some people in favor of the relationship and others against it. Curiously, my grandmother, who was a widow, disagreed with the rest of the family: we're in Brazil, she would say, not Europe—we have to accept that things here are different. The matriarch's opinion was decisive. My parents ended up getting married. And they chose to move to Porto Alegre. There, in the state capital, they would have more opportunities. And they would attract less attention.

So they moved, and from then on it was just work and more work. In the front part of a small house where they lived, in the *Cidade Baixa* district, they opened a small store where they sold Amazonian crafts. The idea was to sell to the Argentine tourists who strolled through the city, and, in fact, they had a pretty good clientele: everything depended on the exchange rate between Brazilian and Argentine currencies, something that my mom got used to keeping track of in the newspaper. Every time there was a devaluation in Brazil she would rub her hands together, pleased. And so they lived, through moments of prosperity and lean times, the latter generally predominating. They had a daughter, Glória, and five years later they had a boy—me. They baptized me Ricardo, but ever since I was little they called me by my nickname, Richie. And Richie I remained. You're Richie, not rich, my sister once said. It was an accusation: I had spent a bunch of money on comic books. Richie, not rich. My mom, who used to try to make peace between us, merely sighed.

And there were reasons for sighing. At the high school where I studied, a private school—that my mom paid for through great sacrifice—I soon figured out that I was different. Because of my somewhat Indian features, and also because of my father: I was the child of a savage. And my nickname, as a consequence, was Little Savage. More than a few times I got into fights with my classmates. More than a few times I went home crying. My mother tried to console me: don't pay attention to them, son, those people are just ignorant.

My father didn't say anything. He suffered on behalf of his son, of course, but he suffered in silence. He was a good man, but quiet, absorbed in his own thoughts. What I most remember about him are the songs that he would softly sing in some strange native language to lull me to sleep, and the stories he would tell me about Uirá, the Amazonian mermaid—and about the Indians that he referred to as my people.

"My people were exterminated in this country," he used to say, bitterly. "The Indians owned everything, the Indians lived well, they had everything that they wanted. Then the white man came, and with him disease, poverty."

I didn't really understand. Not me or anyone else. Uncle Baldo, who also had moved to Porto Alegre and used to visit us once in a while—after all, it was his sister, his niece and nephew—grumbled whenever my father—inevitably—brought up the sad fate of the Indians: here comes the savage again with his speech. That used to infuriate me. A good number of times I told him off, that enormous man with the red nose. He would simply laugh: what do you know, pipsqueak?

I didn't really know anything. About my father, I knew nothing. I decided to learn about the Indians; I read everything I could get hold of. *The Guarani*, by José de Alencar, fascinated me in particular. There I found a heroic, indomitable Indian, an Indian who could very well be the symbol for Brazil. My father wasn't the Guarani. My father didn't walk free through the Amazon forest. Seated in the little shop, he made his fiber baskets, his small

ceramic figures. I was often angered by that passivity, that resignation. I often resented the genetic misfortune of having been
born looking like him and not my mother.

On the day of his thirtieth birthday, my father didn't feel well
and had to be taken to the *Santa Casa* hospital. A few days later
the diagnosis came: liver cancer, quite advanced. His condition
quickly deteriorated, and in just a few weeks he was just skin and
bones. Then he made a request: he wanted to die in his home-
land, in the Amazon, with his people if possible. Crying, my
mother said that it was impossible: my father was in no condition
to travel. Then I want to die in our house, he said. Taking a deep
breath, the doctor authorized his release from the hospital.

His agony was brief, but terrifying. Though stoic, dad would
cry out from the pain. I would cover my ears in order not to hear
it. It was no use; I couldn't sleep. One night I got out of bed and
went to their room. And what I saw was burned into my memory:
there was my mother, walking back and forth across the room—
with my father in her arms. A strong woman, she carried him
almost effortlessly. And she sang softly, so that he would sleep,
one of those indigenous songs. The tears ran down her face, but
she sang, she sang without pause, as if it were a ritual. Three days
later, dad died.

After his death, things got a lot worse at home. Deprived of
our source of income, mom had to get a job. She got a position
as manager of a supermarket. She earned a decent salary, but she
worked a lot, and was always exhausted. She became a bitter,
irritable woman. She fought a lot with my sister who, as soon as
she could, left home to become a flight attendant—and she then
rarely visited. I became the receptacle of maternal hopes—these
included, for me, a brilliant future as a medical doctor, a profession mom greatly admired.

Medicine, however, was not in my plans. I wanted to be an

actor. This desire grew in part from the awareness of my difference. Perhaps out of vengeance, I imitated others—and I did it perfectly. They'd make fun of me? I'd make fun of them. But it wasn't
just that, it was also talent, a talent that my teachers recognized
and encouraged. I was always invited to recite poetry. But I didn't
limit myself to reciting the poems; I also improvised. During a
party celebrating the end of the school year, I recited Gonçalves
Dias, alternating verses with somersaults: "My land has swaying
palms"—somersault. "Where the *sabiá* bird sings"—somersault.
Oh, yeah, and at the part where it says, "The birdsong in this land
is a very different thing," I imitated a bird singing. It was a big hit.
My mother, who was seated in the first row, applauded me, of
course, but she didn't change her opinion: theater was something
for high school kids, not responsible, grown men.

This disagreement was drawn out over years, years during
which I joined and left a good number of amateur theater groups,
without ever really achieving anything concrete, nothing that
would mark me as a professional artist. I would meet a friend of
a friend whose sister-in-law worked with the Globo television
network ... Nothing would come of it, nothing: the sister-in-law
at Globo was no longer there, or she didn't answer her phone,
or she had lost her position of influence. In short, dashed hopes.
Episodes like this were endlessly repeated—with my mother constantly pressuring me: how long are you going to keep up this
foolishness? Finally an idea came to me: to study psychology. I
would choose a course of study that wasn't very demanding, I
would get my degree—satisfying my mother—but, at the same
time, I would dedicate myself to theater.

I took the university entrance exam and passed. It wasn't hard,
and I was an excellent student. I started to go to classes and even
became interested in the subject—after all, theater has a lot to do
with psychology. Soon, however, I discovered that I didn't want
to understand people, I wanted their applause, whether they had

emotional problems or not. I worked with the student drama club, and that helped me to tolerate my studies, even more so because at the time I was having an affair with the director of the group, a fiery forty-something-year-old woman named Inês. Encouraged by her, I decided to drop out and dedicate myself exclusively to theater.

Breaking the news to my mother wasn't easy. It took me weeks to do so, with Inês insisting the whole time that I resolve the situation once and for all. One night, mom and I were having dinner. I mustered my courage.

"Mom, I'm dropping out of college. I don't want to be a psychologist; I want to be an actor."

Her reaction was much worse than I could have imagined. She threw herself onto the couch, crying and screaming. She said I wanted to kill her, that she wouldn't survive the shock. Eventually she even grabbed a framed picture of me—me somersaulting during the school party—she threw it to the floor and began furiously stomping on it.

I was devastated by all that. But I held firm: theater was what I wanted to do, and theater was what I would do, with or without her support. Having made my decision, it was just a matter of moving forward.

Moving forward—but to where? That was the problem. The amateur groups I had worked with kept dispersing, like smoke in the air. Inês, who had encouraged me, traded me in for another young man and took off with him. I also came to the conclusion that I would have to change cities, and I went to Curitiba. There I was recruited by a semi-amateur theater company for a play called *Hamlet in Brasília*. The director, from São Paulo, was Nelson—or Neco to his friends—and he was still young and quite pretentious. He considered himself to be a force for the renewal of Brazilian theater. *Hamlet in Brasília* was an adaptation of Shakespeare's drama, a satire of the political situation in the country. Hamlet was presented as a prince but also as a revolutionary who publicly denounced a palace intrigue. The project had gotten some media coverage, so in fact there were a number of candidates trying out for the role of the Brazilian Hamlet. Without great hopes, I auditioned, and, to my surprise, I was chosen for the starring role.

A role that had its peculiarities, of course, above all during the soliloquy. I had to recite it while undressing myself: "To be or not to be," I would say, and I would take off my shirt. "That is the question," and then off would come the pants. And so on and so forth until I was completely nude. Because, and this must have weighed on the director's choice (who, I think, had a serious crush on me; at least he made certain insinuations), I was easy on the eyes: the indigenous features of my face were at least interesting, I had a good body and was well endowed. So my soliloquy would leave hearts racing among the female members of the audience, helping to add to the box office take.

That was not, unfortunately, what happened. *Hamlet in Brasília* was coolly received. People did show up to see it, but the message was so subliminal that nobody understood it. And my full-frontal nudity aroused some irritation. Chief Shakespeare must be turning in his grave, was one newspaper critic's comment.

For me it was a shock. The review acknowledged my merits ("The young actor, Ricardo, does what he can, struggling against the embarrassing nudity"), but that was hardly the beginning for a very promising career. Timidly, I suggested to Nelson that we change the focus of the play. Who knows, maybe returning a bit to the original text . . . ?

His response was fury, and disdain. Just as uptight on the stage as in bed, I'm sure. We're not going to change anything. If you want, you can quit. There's no shortage of substitutes for you.

I ended up apologizing, which was humiliating. And the worst was yet to come.

One day I got a call from Porto Alegre: my mother. Crying, she said she missed me terribly—and regretted having rejected my vocation. She asked me to forgive her for that. And she had news.

"I know you're performing in a play there in Curitiba. I want to see you on stage. I already bought a bus ticket."

That was just what I needed, my mom in the audience for a play in which I appeared in the nude. I tried everything I could to dissuade her from coming: it wasn't worth it, the run of the play was already wrapping up (which was true, by the way). And the trip was long, uncomfortable—it would be better for me to go to Porto Alegre to see her.

All of my arguments were useless: two days later, she arrived in Curitiba. I went to meet her at the bus station. Our reunion was, of course, moving; she asked for forgiveness, I asked for forgiveness, the two of us crying the whole time.

"I can't wait to see you perform," mom said.

She asked if I could get her a ticket for that same night.

"But you must be tired," I suggested.

"I couldn't be less tired," she responded. "I want to be there cheering you on."

I left her at the hotel and went directly to speak with Nelson. It was almost noon, but he was still sleeping. I had to wait for him to wake up—he hated having his sleep interrupted—and then, with the guy still half asleep and ill-humored, I told him that my mother was coming. I explained that the nude scene would be a shock for her; couldn't I, as an exception, perform the soliloquy dressed, or at least with my underwear on?

Nelson—and I think there was even a bit of sadism involved, some vengeance for my not having fallen into his arms as others had done before—was intransigent: art cannot be compromised by these bourgeois allergies.

I left furious—and desperate. What could I do? I began to think about taking off, quitting the play once and for all. On the other hand, that would amount to a tremendous lack of consideration for my mom, who, after all, had made this trip in order to see her son—and to reconcile with him and to prove to him that she was accepting his choice to go into theater. After much vacillation, I decided to warn her about what she would see that night: you know, modern theater takes certain liberties, don't be alarmed.

That was what I did. Before the show, I went to pick her up at the hotel, and on the way to the theater I began to explain to her what was going to happen. It didn't do any good. She didn't listen to me, or, if she did, she paid no mind. She wanted to see her son on stage and that was that. She wanted to applaud for him. And she was happy, very happy. Resigned, I prepared myself for the disaster.

And a disaster it was, a much bigger disaster than I imagined. Seated in the first row, mom clapped deliriously when I came on stage. She applauded so much and so slowly that other members of the audience had to ask her to be quiet. She watched me, ecstatic.

Then came the scene with the soliloquy. I took off my pants—still okay. It's in God's hands now, I thought. I took a deep breath and tore off my underpants. My mother did not hesitate even an instant; she got up and, stepping on the feet of the other spectators, left. I didn't know what to do; only with tremendous effort was I able to stay on the stage. The curtain had barely dropped, and I got dressed and rushed over to the modest hotel where she was staying.

"She said that she doesn't want to speak with anyone," the man at the front desk told me, a fat guy who was chewing on a toothpick.

"But she's my mother," I insisted. "I need to speak with her."

He frowned.

"I don't care if you're her son or not. Didn't you hear: she doesn't want to talk with anybody. Now get out of here."

I left concerned. What would mom do? She would likely catch the first bus back, I thought, but I was wrong. Unfortunately.

The following night, among the few people in the audience, whom do I see? My mother, extremely stiff in her seat, in the same spot in the first row. My first reaction was one of happiness: I thought that, after spending the night thinking about it, she had come to the conclusion that that's what theater was, that talent had nothing to do with nudity. She was there to support me. Again, I was wrong.

When the moment for the soliloquy came, mom stood up, removed from her purse some sort of black blindfold, which she secured over her eyes. And there she remained, standing, turned toward the stage, that tall, sturdy woman, her eyes blindfolded. A protest that surprised everyone, in part and primarily because she repeated it the following night.

At that point the thing had caught the media's attention. Television crews came, newspapers came—mother protesting against her son, the actor, was one of the headlines—and the audience grew, now out of curiosity. Nelson was extremely happy; finally we had some ticket sales. For weeks he had tried to come up with something that would attract attention to the play. He had sent anonymous letters to the newspapers saying that the character of the king, denounced by Hamlet, alluded to the interior minister. He hoped that this would create some sort of rebuttal—in fact, his wish was for the minister to press charges against him, making him a martyr for freedom of expression. But the letters simply weren't published, and the minister, it seemed, had other things to do. Now, however, mom had solved the problem: there was a reason for people to come to the play. And this, for Nelson, was fantastic.

I, however, felt more depressed than ever. My mother simply refused to see me. She wouldn't see me at the hotel, she wouldn't answer the phone. What she wanted to do was just that: demonstrate her discontent with her ingrate son. All this left me at wit's end. One night, I let Nelson know: this is my last performance, you can find another Hamlet. He tried to convince me to change my mind. There was an argument, and I ended up hitting him in the face a couple of times.

That night, mom didn't show up. Without saying goodbye, she had left. And I was left there to face an unsettling, painful question: What do I do with my life now?

5

ADAMASTOR MAKES HIS PROPOSAL, DECENT OR INDECENT

The following afternoon I had an answer.

I was napping in the tiny room in the miserable boardinghouse where I lived when the landlady (ill-humoredly: I hadn't paid my rent in weeks) knocked at the door.

"There's a man here. He wants to talk to you."

A man wanting to talk to me? What man? I didn't know anyone—nor did I want to know anyone. It must be some old queen, I thought—it wasn't uncommon for theater actors, especially the young ones, and especially the failed ones, to be sought out by those types. My first reaction was to respond that I didn't want to see anyone. But the truth is that I was so upset, I felt so abandoned, that any visitor, queer or not, would do me some good.

I went down to the living room and there was Adamastor. He introduced himself, very cordial, said he was in Curitiba on business (in fact, as I later discovered, he had come to buy building materials), and, taking advantage of the opportunity, had decided to go to the theater, something he hadn't done for a long time.

"I did not regret my decision," he said. "I liked the play a lot. Truth is, I saw it twice."

Twice? How strange. There were people who left halfway through *Hamlet in Brasília*. But seeing it twice? Peculiar. Okay, I felt flattered, a compliment from an audience member always massages the ego—in my case, it was quite needed—but that extravagant passion for the play made me suspicious. He wanted something from me. And he wasn't hitting on me. The man, in a suit and tie, very composed, seemed more like an executive at a business meeting—not even the ponytail seemed out of place, he could have been a hip businessman. So I left diplomacy aside and got straight to the point.

"I thank you for the compliments. But I don't think you came here just to comment on my performance. Am I right?"

He shifted in his chair, a bit embarrassed, and said that, as a matter of fact, he had a proposal for me. Then he told me about the project, Eden-Brazil, and about the play: a modest production, just a half-hour long (but repeated a number of times throughout the day) and perhaps unworthy of my talents, but it was part of a larger project, something unprecedented in Brazil, a revolutionary undertaking. He asked if I wanted to be Adam.

It might have been a sham, like so many others in the world of the arts, and normally I would turn down the offer, even if no longer to protect the scant artistic dignity I had remaining in me. But the truth is I was impressed by Adamastor. Madness, his proposal? And what if? *Hamlet in Brasília* was also half mad and, even worse, madness that hadn't worked. Moreover, what did I have to lose? I was nothing more than an unemployed actor; truth is, if I wanted food and shelter, I would have to depend on my mother—who would hold it over me for the rest of my life, every single crumb: I told you this theater stuff wasn't serious, but no, you didn't listen, you never listen, you preferred to venture off on your own and look what it got you, you don't have a job, you don't have a degree, you don't have anything, you even need me to feed you. In this Eden-Brazil I would have, free from the sermons, food and shelter. On the Santa Catarina coast, which was nothing to turn up your nose at.

But still I wavered. Would my fate be to exhibit myself, nude, in a theater or in a theme park? Couldn't I come up with anything better? What would the famous actor, Paulo Autran, do if he were in my shoes? Or Raul Cortez, or Antônio Fagundes? Would they accept an offer like this?

Noticing my indecision, Adamastor extended an invitation.

"Come see the place," he said. "Be my guest for a week. There, with a better sense of the project, you'll see I'm right," he guaranteed. "If you don't like it, I'll pay for your return ticket. By plane."

Well, that was reasonable. I was in.

6

I START TO GET INTO THE
SPIRIT OF THINGS

The next day, at seven in the morning, there he was, parked in front of the boardinghouse. As we were leaving, there was an incident. The landlady didn't want to let me leave without paying the back rent. I promised that I was just about to start a new job and that soon I would be able to settle the debt, with interest even. But she would have none of it:

"I'm sick of promises. Especially promises made by artists. You're nothing but a bunch of liars. If you don't pay up, you're not leaving."

Duly backed up by her employee, a *mulatto* who stood over six feet tall, she blocked the door. Adamastor, who was waiting in the car, came to find out what was going on. When he learned what the problem was, he wrote out a check for the amount the woman was demanding while I, confused, tried to protest: "What are you doing, Adamastor? You shouldn't do that."

But he neutralized my discomfort with the situation with one kind phrase: "Take this as a vote of confidence. It's payment for your release."

Finally, we departed. During the trip, we talked, excitedly. He ended up telling me about his life, and I told him about mine. And then we climbed the road that led to the top of the mountain, and there, before me, was that astounding panoramic view. I had been to the Santa Catarina coast before; I had spent an entire summer there with a group of friends. They were weeks spent drinking and partying, but, even so, the beauty of the place stuck in my memory. Now Adamastor's beach surpassed all of my expectations. He had not exaggerated: it was truly like paradise.

He put me up in his own house and treated me very well. He wanted me to get to know Eden-Brazil, and that's what I did: for a week I walked through the jungle, ran on the beach, swam in the sea. Diving into the warm water, I concluded that even if it all turned out to be a failure, it would be better to fail in an idyllic locale than in a decaying theater in some city. So, one night, during dinner, I said I would accept the proposal. He was elated: I knew you would agree, you're already imbued with the spirit of the thing.

The next day, he introduced me to Gutiérrez. The Argentine looked me up and down and approved, mainly because of the features I had inherited from my father. I would give a touch of authenticity to the production. A Brazilian Adam, from the point of view of the foreign press (Gutiérrez was already thinking about promoting the show abroad), would be great.

So, they already had the actor, but just the actor. Everything else was missing: the director, the actress for the role of Eve, the script. Gutiérrez asked if I knew anyone with talent and imagination who could direct the play. I told him about a friend of mine (not the director of *Hamlet in Brasília*; I didn't want anything to do with him ever again), a guy named Paulo who quickly agreed to meet with us. Adamastor sent him a plane ticket; apparently money was not a problem for him, which gave everything an added appeal that, even if I wasn't a sellout, I couldn't help but acknowledge. He went to pick him up at the airport in Florianópolis, and, as he did with me, he set him up in his house, which was large enough to accommodate a lot of people. Right away, that night, there the three of us were, talking over the details of the production.

Short, with glasses, the face of an intellectual, Paulo was just a bit older than me; unlike me, he was a guy who was easily excited. Just as I had foreseen, he immediately fell in love with the project. He saw in it unlimited—and revolutionary—possibilities.

"This traditional, indoor theater stuff is outdated. The thing now is to perform in places like prisons, hospitals, asylums—or in the jungle, like we're going to do here."

During our meetings, we talked excitedly, Paulo, Gutiérrez, and me, but Adamastor didn't say anything. Suddenly he seemed a bit estranged from the process, which made me feel a bit bad— and apprehensive: I was afraid that eventually he would get fed up and give up on the production. But then his interest returned— and in an unexpected way. It was when we began to discuss who would play the role of Eve. Paulo had two proposals: either we would invite a known actress or we would hold public auditions. This second alternative would have the benefit of drawing public attention to the project: no doubt the media would give good coverage to such an original competition. And then Adamastor announced that he would make the choice for Eve. As a matter of fact, he had someone in mind for the role: a niece, Isabel, a young woman—eighteen years old—who, according to him, had a lot of talent for the theater.

The news, frankly, left us all concerned. Obviously, Adamastor had the right to some influence in the selection of the actress, after all, he was the one who was paying for everything. But this wasn't an appropriate situation for nepotism: we needed talent, not family ties. Even worse, it seemed a bit strange that he would think of a niece for a role that, because of the nudity, would certainly shock some people—no matter how artistic the production was. That was what Paulo and I were pondering. But the guy proved to be unshakeable; he wanted his niece to be Eve. Which left us suspicious. Was she really his niece, or some girlfriend? But, in that case, why would he hide it? And why would he put the girl in a play in which she would have to appear in the nude? Were we dealing with some strange exhibitionist?

It didn't seem so. His belief in the project, even to the point of naivety, was proof of his sincerity. Yes, he knew that the scene required nudity, but it would be pure, innocent nudity. Paulo tried other arguments to dissuade him: wouldn't her parents be upset at seeing their daughter as Eve?

"Don't worry about that," was Adamastor's curt response. "She's an orphan."

It was no use. We agreed, and Adamastor telephoned his niece, who lived in the capital, asking her to come. When she arrived, I was absolutely sure there would be problems. She was very pretty, Isabel: a blond with big blue eyes, full lips, and a perfect body. Good lord, with that Eve how could Adam not sink into anguished temptation—especially an Adam like me, who hadn't been with a woman for some time. But my stage experience, even if limited, had taught me that it's not always a good idea to mix work and romance, primarily if it involved the boss's "niece"—the quotation marks indicate the suspicions I had. So, conversation between us was kept absolutely neutral. She said things that were typical for someone who was just starting out in the theater (I always wanted to be an actress, the stage is my life); I, supposedly more experienced, encouraged her (I think you're going to have a great career), and that's how things stayed. I wanted to maintain some distance between us, but, unfortunately for me (and, for his convenience, I imagined), Adamastor also put her up in his house. Isabel's room was at the end of a long hallway, far from mine. Closer, of course, to her "uncle's" room. I tried to ignore whatever was going on and pay no attention to nocturnal sounds like footsteps in the hallway, whispers, cries, and moans of pleasure. But I can't deny that I listened intently and had a hard time sleeping.

The adaptation of Genesis that Paulo came up with was faithful to the original biblical text. Adamastor's request.

"I'm worried that some religious guy is going to pick a fight with us," he explained, and his concern soon would prove to be absolutely prophetic.

It was a simple script. Adam and Eve were presented as two innocent children, in thrall to nature. Little by little, however, they discover each other, the forbidden fruit being the expression of this love.

With the script ready and approved by Adamastor, we did our first reading. This was, in short, a painful experience. The problem was Isabel. It wasn't just a question of inexperience, which was immediately evident: she stumbled over words, she sometimes stuttered. But that could be corrected. The problem was her ill humor, which was soon evident. In the middle of the reading she threw her copy of the script to the ground.

"It won't work. No way. It won't work."

We said nothing, taken aback.

"What's wrong, Isabel?" Paulo asked. "Are you not feeling well?"

"I'm fine," she responded in a sarcastic tone. "What's not fine is your script."

"What's wrong with the script?"

"It's a piece of shit, don't you see? A piece of shit. This Eve of yours is an idiot. I've never seen such a stupid woman. She doesn't understand anything about anything. And to top it off, it makes it seem as if she's a temptress. She's not. She's a moron."

"How would you like Eve to be?" asked Paulo, his brow furrowed.

Isabel explained at length: her character should be a determined woman. Aware of the risks of transgression, she still wished to assume them.

"She loses Paradise, sure. As a matter of fact, it seems Paradise was exactly like Eden-Brazil: boring, someplace where nothing happens—so Eve would have to take the initiative. It has to be clear that, between the two of them, she's the one who had the courage to change. That Adam didn't do anything, apart from donating that rib—another story that I think is poorly told."

Paulo and I tried to argue that the play was not intended to contest anything: we simply wanted to discuss the idea of Paradise. But Isabel held fast to her opinions. Each day, each rehearsal, she was less and less cooperative—rather, she was authoritarian. And, worse still, she evidently had some growing influence on her "uncle" (with or without quotation marks: I still didn't know). Adamastor, who always showed up for rehearsals, appeared increasingly concerned with the changes proposed by Isabel. This was what he suggested, in the most diplomatic way possible:

"Listen, Isabel, don't you think it's better to follow Paulo's directions? After all, he is the director of the play. Moreover, he's simply following the Bible. I don't know if these innovations are going to go over very well . . ."

"I could care less," she said, acerbic. "I already told you: if you want me here, things have to be done according to my rules. Is that clear?"

"It is," said Adamastor, in a hushed, strained voice.

Paulo and I uncomfortably witnessed the scene (I was even more uncomfortable since I was naked). Adamastor had clearly been humiliated, but all he did was remain silent. At that very moment Gutiérrez arrived. Isabel recounted for him the discussion, telling him about the changes she was proposing. To our surprise, Gutiérrez appeared enthusiastic, even close to ecstatic.

"Brilliant, Isabel! Brilliant! You've introduced an element of contestation into the Bible itself!"

"This is going to cause controversy," warned Paulo, who was a competent director, though to a certain extent also conventional: for him, theater shouldn't be transformed into a pamphlet, whether feminist or of any other sort.

"Great," replied Gutiérrez. "Controversy is exactly what I want. The more debate the production provokes, the more media stories, the better. Better for you, better for Eden-Brazil."

He heartily congratulated Isabel and paid her any number of compliments—which, I noticed, left dear uncle a bit bothered. Other discussions of the same sort followed, but finally we got back to the script. It was about thirty minutes long, which, according to Gutiérrez, was the ideal amount of time for the production. After all, the tourists wouldn't be coming to Eden-Brazil for theater. And, moreover, they would have to watch the play while standing, so it shouldn't be very long.

So, we had a script, we had a director, an actor, an actress. One thing was missing.

The snake.

The snake was the object of much discussion. It was, naturally, essential for the temptation scene; but using a live snake would be a problem. A monkey could be trained, a dog too. But reptiles are notoriously unpredictable. Yes, there are snake charmers, but where would we find one, in Brazil? And what snake charmer would be able to convince a serpent to perform every day with an apple in its mouth? Finally, Paulo had an idea, an idea he was immediately excited about. We wouldn't use a real snake, but instead a prop—a robot, to be more precise—moved by remote control.

"The public adores those types of special effects. And it will make our lives easier."

Adamastor didn't like the idea. He didn't want a fake animal in a project that was intended to show nature in its authenticity. Paulo argued that theater and film were ever more dependent on technology. But that is the evil of our times, Adamastor protested, to which Paulo retorted: and wasn't the serpent, after all, the symbol of evil?

The discussion went on for hours and assuredly would have gone on even longer if Isabel had been there. She wasn't. Once in a while she borrowed Adamastor's car under the pretext of buying something in the village (though it wasn't very far away) and disappeared. The other person who wasn't at the meeting—and should have been—was Gutiérrez. Adamastor decided to call him. They talked about the debate they were having. Gutiérrez, who in general was not a man of few words, including and primarily when he was on the phone, was, on this occasion, notably brief. In half a minute, Adamastor was hanging up the phone.

"He thinks Paulo's idea is a good one," he said. I couldn't help notice the expression of displeasure on his face. I thought he seemed offended by Gutiérrez, but I didn't want to ask. It was none of my business, nor was it the time.

Paulo, though, was quite satisfied with Gutiérrez's support.

"That guy really knows his stuff, Adamastor. You did well by hiring him."

He called up a friend, an electronics engineer who specialized in projects for the theater. The man accepted the challenge. He wouldn't come cheap—but by that time we already knew that Adamastor would pay whatever was necessary.

Two weeks later, the engineer brought the serpent for a

demonstration. And even Adamastor had to admit it was a mas-
terpiece. It was large—more than six feet long. So it will be quite
visible, as the engineer said. Though made out of plastic, it looked
real—so much so that Lucifer, perched on Adamastor's shoulder,
had a panic attack and, screaming, fled inside the house. This left
Gutiérrez pleased. It's the voice of nature, he commented.

Powered by batteries and operated by remote control, the
snake was made up of dozens of mobile, articulated parts. So
it could slither, it could climb trees, it could open and close its
mouth—in short, it could do anything a snake does. The eyes
were miniature cameras, allowing for the person operating the
snake to have a view onto what was happening. And the serpent
spoke; the engineer had equipped it for this as well. It contained
a chip with a recording made by Dóris Souza, a famous television
actress, considered a sex symbol. The text was long. First, the
serpent talked about the forbidden fruit. Why, it asked, should
knowledge of Good and Evil remain hidden within a fruit that
neither Adam nor Eve could eat? What in this fruit benefited
from such knowledge? The seeds? Well? Do the seeds, by chance,
say to each other that beauty is Good and ugliness is Evil? Is that
the purpose of seeds, to ramble on about Good and Evil? As a
matter of fact, why have seeds in a fruit that can't be eaten? Why
this waste of organic material, so incompatible with the extreme
rationality of the divine creator?

This monologue, however, made apparent the ambivalence
of the serpent itself, an ambivalence that was translated into
brusque movements of its head, first to the right, now to the left.
Speaking to the forbidden fruit, which obviously didn't respond,
the serpent was, in fact, sustaining an interior dialogue. It was
speaking of its own ambivalence. The ambivalence that anticipated that of humans, and that itself had been anticipated by that

of the forbidden fruit, with its dual and dialectical potentiality: Good and Evil (or, perhaps, Digested and Undigested, but this is to speak of another dimension, the material, rather than the spiritual; the physiological dimension, the pathological dimension, the dimension of food safety, the dimension of consumer protection protocols). What is certain is that, distinct from the fruit, the serpent made its choice. The fruit: dual proposal, one thing or the other. The serpent: a single proposal, the proposal that, in a smooth, sultry, sensual voice (but one not completely free of anxiety, okay? Not completely free of anxiety), she would make to the first woman. Who, more or less according to the Bible, would react with timid surprise: Not that one, serpent, we can eat any fruit but that one there, or else Adam and I will die. Forget that, the serpent would say, you won't die at all; to the contrary, you will be like God, you will discover things that you've never even imagined. Life isn't just this monotonous Paradise; life can be full of surprises, some good, others not so good, but the truth is you need to take a risk, you need to have ambitions, you need to think big, sometimes you even need to transgress, because a little bit of transgression is good for you. Those who forever stay on the straight and narrow are boring. Don't you know that the future belongs to those who take risks? And then the serpent would describe to the stunned Eve a world full of the marvels science and technology would provide: Have you ever thought of flying, Eve? Have you ever thought about speaking with Adam across long distances? Have you ever thought about illuminating the dark nights with something that doesn't yet exist, but that certainly will come to exist and that will be called the electric light bulb? Then followed brief yet convincing descriptions of things such as the microwave oven, radio, and television. With Eve convinced, or almost convinced, the serpent plucked with its coils the said fruit (an apple; despite well-known disagreements as to the type of fruit, Adamastor had chosen the version consecrated by folklore) and offered it to Eve.

Adamastor didn't much like the dialogue between the serpent and the forbidden fruit. What's this about a snake talking to an apple? It's metaphorical, Paulo explained.

"The serpent introduces temptation, but not just carnal temptation. The temptation of the comfortable life of the middle class—that's exactly what you want to change. I don't see a problem with the snake talking to the apple. Didn't you want to see your visitors talking to the flowers? It's the same thing."

They discussed it for a long time, and finally Adamastor made a proposal: this would be the only innovation. The rest of the text would stay faithful to the Bible. Paulo, who was an agreeable sort, happily agreed to the proposal.

Okay, but who would operate the robotic snake? It wasn't something that just anyone would be capable of. The engineer agreed. But he had someone in mind for the task: one of his assistants, Macedo. He can be counted on, he guaranteed, and he's trained to make any repairs that may be necessary.

Adamastor accepted the proposal, and two days later Macedo showed up. He was a skinny kid with bad posture and a somewhat vacant gaze that didn't much impress Adamastor.

"This kid looks like he was just released from a psychiatric hospital."

Despite Adamastor's reservations, it soon became apparent that Macedo was an expert in remote control. In his hands, the serpent (nicknamed by him Maria Angélica, perhaps in homage to an old girlfriend—if in fact he had ever had a girlfriend before) was capable of the most extraordinary performances. Macedo made it execute, to mark the beginning of the scene of temptation, a fantastic ballet that left everyone, including Adamastor, holding their breath. Gutiérrez couldn't be more pleased; Paulo was ecstatic, commenting that the serpent alone would guarantee the success of any show. Hired, Macedo was given a room, though a smaller one (the hierarchy needed to be maintained), in Adamastor's house.

We didn't have any problems with God either.

Yes, God. Jehovah. He was also one of the characters.

From the beginning, it had been clear—to all of us—that we did not want to personify him. In the first place, this would mean another actor: some old guy with a white beard, like the one on the Sistine Chapel. For all of us, it would be uncomfortable to live with an entity like that. Moreover, introducing God wouldn't be easy. He couldn't stand on the ground like Adam and Eve, nor could he hang from a tree like the serpent. He would have to be up high, levitating, which would require hoists or other, more complicated equipment (a small helicopter and a platform?). Monumental costs, a thousand problems . . . No way. God, for us, would be a voice. That's all: a voice. Now, it would have to be a very special voice, a voice that would truly convey the idea of divine omnipotence and omniscience.

And that voice, fortunately, we soon found; it was the voice of Fernando Porto, a well-known radio broadcaster. A friend of Gutiérrez, he spent his vacations in Santa Catarina, and he agreed to make us a recording of the voice of the God of Genesis. For someone who read out news of catastrophes, terror attacks, and wars, it wasn't hard. It wasn't exactly pleasant either. It was something much, much more than that. It was sublime—the term used by Fernando Porto himself. He told us that this had always been a dream of his: to lend his voice to a transcendent figure—and who is more transcendent than God?

The recording wasn't something to be done just off the cuff. It demanded real preparation. Porto, a serious professional, presented to us—in writing—a sort of descriptive prospectus for the work he planned to develop. The voice of God, it stated, must be constituted by the radiophonic reflection of an image that has determined the fortunes of humanity since the prehistoric era, the image of divinity. The voice of God must be neutral without being monotonous; it must be energetic without being authoritarian. The voice of God must be deep, like the notes from a cathedral organ. The speech must be measured, without recourse to melodramatic tricks such as affected moments of suspense.

"Go for it," said Gutiérrez, after scanning the document. The recording was made in a studio in Florianópolis. At Fernando Porto's request, we were all there—he wanted feedback on his performance.

And it was a great performance. Carefully containing the emotion—he was great at that—Porto read the text in an impeccable manner. When it came to an end, we all effusively complimented him. How much do I owe you? asked Adamastor. Nothing, said Porto, this recording wasn't work, it was a glory bestowed. I should be paying you. Adamastor insisted, but he stood firm: no payment necessary. He just made one demand: he did not want his name divulged. He was worried about fanatics: they might think that I've tried to adopt not just the voice of God but also his powers, and then I would most certainly be in danger. Gutiérrez guaranteed strict anonymity. The voice would also be somewhat disguised by the use of an echo chamber, the purpose of which was to present the voice of God as resounding throughout the vastness of the world, but that also resulted in a providential bit of distortion.

We began to rehearse. Together with Adamastor, Paulo had already chosen the site for the performance: a small clearing in the middle of the forest, a shady spot conveniently circled by a sparse bamboo grove. The visitors would arrive by foot via a trail and there they would stop to watch the show through the bamboo. That's exactly the emotional ambience that I want, said Paulo, the emotional ambience of a voyeur watching a forbidden scene.

"The audience will feel like it's part of the transgression."

An interesting idea, but for me it felt strange. I was used to looking at the faces of the audience for signs of approval or rejection (preferably approval, of course). Now, however, the audience would be invisible; I would have to imagine the people behind the bamboo. Which would assuredly be cause for continual uncertainty: Is that thing over there I'm seeing an eye shining with emotion or just the sun's reflection on a wet leaf? Is what I heard the murmurs of admiration or the rustling of plants?

But that was a relatively small problem. What really bothered me—and I was bothered that it bothered me—was something else. I couldn't understand my character, Adam.

The Bible doesn't say much about him. It doesn't describe him physically. It doesn't say what he did, how he would spend his time. We know he didn't have to work or get up early, that his day was a mystery; but not even things he said are mentioned (not to mention something like an internal monologue). What was it like, after all, to be the first man? What was it like to look around and not see a single colleague from work, or a guy you play sports with, or a fellow member of a political party? What was it like to not have a father, or a mother, or siblings? What was it like to have direct access to the divine, to hear its thundering voice? It was impossible to inhabit the skin of a character like this. Sometimes he seemed to me a moron, a happy fool; at other times, I saw him as a mysterious, enigmatic being. And, not infrequently, I thought of him as someone who was continually perplexed. Like he was helpless. Just as I had felt helpless standing before my father's coffin, a constant—and vivid—memory. At some point, the pain had subsided a bit, giving way not to resignation but to a sort of melancholy curiosity: what was it like to be dead, I asked myself, staring at my father, my vision still clouded by tears.

Adam might have asked questions like that, though not while crying. I couldn't imagine him crying. Nor laughing. Nor swearing. Nor singing. I couldn't imagine him—that was that. Adam, for me, was insipid, with no color or smell. Of course, for the audience this would make no difference. They weren't coming here in search of complexity. They would come in search of simple pleasures. They would come seeking Adam, the simpleton. But since I was a complicated guy, how could I play the part of a simple character?

Isabel had no similar concerns. For her, everything was great; the script had been changed according to her wishes, naturally, but even apart from that, she was quite content, laughing for no reason, something that even the perpetually distracted Paulo noticed.

"Something's changed with that girl. I wonder what."

I didn't respond. But I had my suspicions, which I kept to myself since it really wasn't the time to talk about them: the day of the premier was quickly arriving.

The first rehearsal naturally took place in secret. Isabel, myself, Gutiérrez, Paulo, Macedo. And Adamastor—hidden behind the bamboo; he wanted to feel like someone from our (future) audience watching the play. Isabel wore only a robe. I couldn't wait for the moment for her to take it off—and at the same time, I was nervous about that moment.

Paulo asked us to take our places. A musical introduction, specially prepared, solemnly resonated through the grove. I took a deep breath and took off my robe. Isabel did the same, and, oh God, her body was absolutely stunning. With extraordinary effort, I was able to control myself. Even so, my first line ("Eva, what are you doing over there?") came out in something like a shriek, which made both Gutiérrez and Paulo smile. But I continued on. As we had anticipated, Isabel proved to be a mediocre actress; but she would do. At least now she said her lines more naturally, without forgetting any of them.

The grand sensation was the serpent. It truly seemed alive, moving with unbelievable precision. As for the lighting and sound effects, they were both fine. The voice of Dóris Souza lecherously echoed through the forest, which was, by the way, a wonderful stage for the production. Oh yeah, and the voice of God was an excellent counterpoint.

In sum, we wrapped up the rehearsal all quite satisfied. Gutiérrez was even euphoric, saying that rarely had he seen such an excellent production; he hugged and kissed Isabel (who still had no clothes on) repeatedly.

Adamastor was strangely reserved, which heightened the unsettled sense I had about things; something was going on. It bothered me. Because I liked Adamastor. His almost naïve belief in the project moved me. I would be pretty upset if something happened that shook that belief. And something would happen, that was my intuition.

But it wasn't time for intuitions. It was time for optimism, for enthusiasm. Soon we would be showing to the world our vision of Paradise.

7

EDEN-BRAZIL OPENS TO THE WORLD, THOUGH WITHOUT THE RECIPROCAL BEING TRUE

We were ready to start. The hotel, almost finished, could accommodate a reasonable number of guests. But access was terrible because of the poorly maintained, narrow dirt road. Adamastor and Gutiérrez requested a meeting with the mayor, Argemiro. They showed him the project, pictures of the place, of the hotel. They didn't tell him about the play. Gutiérrez, who knew the man, had advised Adamastor not to mention it; the mayor wasn't really a fan of the theater, especially experimental theater. In any case, Argemiro wasn't interested in such details; he only wanted to know if Eden-Brazil (he liked the name a lot) would attract tourists. Gutiérrez promised that it would. With the bureaucratic hurdles overcome, the town really did do its part, paving those few miles of road. The entrance to Eden-Brazil was now marked by an imposing gate, buttressed by giant billboards praising the excellent qualities of this Brazilian paradise. All of this was Gutiérrez's idea. He also tried to turn the inauguration into an event capable of attracting media attention. For this, he contacted politicians, businessmen, journalists. Adamastor had to pay for full-page ads in a number of the region's newspapers, but he got a lot of support. He was invited onto radio and television programs. He wasn't very good in front of the cameras or microphones; he had to be prepared for this by Gutiérrez himself. He should talk, with an air of mystery, about the "element of surprise" in our Eden-Safari. And this in fact spurred the curiosity of a lot of people, judging by the number of letters the radios and newspapers received.

When the park was inaugurated, there was a modest crowd, despite the light rain that was falling. The mayor showed up, of course, along with a number of city council members. Radio and television journalists were there. In short, a better than decent turnout.

Adamastor, nervous, was running from one place to the next, worrying about details. Now Gutiérrez, dressed in a brightly colored shirt, acted like he was in charge of the show. He even gave a speech in a mixture of Portuguese and Spanish during the cocktail reception—at the end of which people were taken on the guided tour. And then we performed the play—not in the clearing, of course, due to the rain (in the future, we'll have to make arrangements for a canopy, Gutiérrez commented), but on an improvised stage in the hotel ballroom. Before we began, Paulo appeared, introduced himself as the director, and said: "What you are about to see, ladies and gentlemen, is what we might call a modern version of a Bible story. A postmodern vision of Genesis."

If by this he meant to shape the audience's expectations, he was sorely mistaken. When the curtained was raised, revealing Isabel and myself in the nude, eyes widened and jaws dropped. And I could hear clearly the murmurs of shock—and indignation. I was already accustomed to this, but I was afraid that Isabel would be upset. No, she seemed completely at ease on the stage, even satisfied with the commotion she was provoking. She messed up a line or two, but that was more or less to be expected. In any case, what we said was of little interest. It was our nudity that was of interest.

As for me, frankly I was worried, almost panicked. I already had enough stage experience not to let it show, but I had to make use of absolutely all of my capacity for self-control. And I prayed that the serpent, entering the scene, would divert a bit of the audience's attention, and that did in fact happen, but no snake, no matter how ingenious it was, could soften the impact of the scene. It was a relief when, with Adam and Eve finally exiled from Paradise, the curtain fell. I was sweating buckets, agonizing. Isabel, on the other hand, was euphoric: they were blown away, they'd never seen anything like it.

After the show, there was a cocktail reception for the guests. I quickly got dressed and mixed with the crowd, trying to gauge opinions. But of course nobody would speak frankly with me; all I heard were some vague praises. "It's a bit heavy," said the mayor, but that was a relatively benign reaction given the fact that it came from someone known to be conservative. Equally vague were the comments in the next day's newspapers. "Interesting," "creative" were the most repeated judgments, and they didn't necessarily indicate approval.

But that was the good news. The bad news came a few days later. The show, we later discovered, had scandalized a good number of people. Letters from indignant readers appeared in the newspapers. "It's worse than the nudity on the beaches," one of them said. Others lamented the fact that censorship was no longer permitted; one man even spoke nostalgically of the period of the military dictatorship, "when those responsible for trash like this would rot in prison." And then the League for the Defense of Morals got involved.

It was an obscure institution organized by older women residents of a small town on the coast. By one of those unlucky turns of fate, the league's president, *Senhora* Arminda, saw the performance—and she was deeply offended. She didn't even stay for cocktails; she went straight home, where she telephoned her friends, calling a special meeting of the league. The turnout was tremendous. *Senhora* Arminda told of what she had seen ("Shameless, my friends, you can't even imagine"), and she demanded they take a public position on the issue. The women of the league were outraged—and incredibly pleased. This was a real issue. It had been a long time since they had had such a good cause around which to rally; at most, they had protested against the excesses of the region's Carnival celebrations or against some slightly more provocative photograph published in the paper. But the nudity in the play was a true cause to which they could dedicate their free time, of which there was no shortage.

They unanimously decided to wage a holy war against what they considered a den of perdition. To begin with, they hired boys to hand out pamphlets on the road leading to Eden-Brazil. "An Affront to Decent Behavior," was the title. A passage: "The promoters baptized the place with the name Eden-Brazil. They should change the name: Eden it is most certainly not. What it is, rather, is Hell, a redoubt of debased sinners who only want to induce people to temptation." And they went to the newspapers and radio and television stations. They convinced some city counselors to make inflamed speeches. One of them accused the mayor of "supporting concupiscence" with public money, causing a bit of a problem: the other counselors didn't know the meaning of the obscure word.

But all that was nothing. One morning, the guy in charge of the gate came rushing into the house out of breath. Adamastor wasn't there, so the man came directly to my room.

"Excuse me, Mr. Ricardo, but you have to come to the main entrance. Right now."

"What happened?" I was still half asleep.

"Go and see for yourself."

I went. And there was Arminda and another five of her fellow league members, laying down on the road, impeding passage to two cars full of tourists, honking and impatient. I went to speak with the woman.

"Excuse me, but you are blocking traffic."

From the ground, she directed at me a look of anger and disgust.

"Then call the police. Let them arrest me. Then the whole country will learn about our protest."

There was nothing we could do. They didn't leave until it was dark out. By then the visitors had already given up.

It was too much. We had a meeting, Paulo, Adamastor, and I (Gutiérrez said he couldn't come, that he was busy, and Isabel had disappeared). We had a long discussion. I was extremely irritated, and I could only think about ways to get back at the woman, but Paulo, who was a level-headed guy, calmed me down: this fight is of no interest to us, we can only lose.

"What do you suggest, then?" I asked.

"Negotiation. Adamastor has to talk with this *Senhora* Arminda."

We turned toward Adamastor, who listened to us in silence.

"So, Adamastor? Are you up for it?"

He sighed.

"What can we do? We have to do what we have to do. And right away."

He asked me to phone the woman.

"You begin by apologizing. Then pass me the phone."

I thought it too much of a concession. But, to satisfy Adamastor, I found her number in the telephone book, and I called.

The maid answered. I heard her telling the woman that "the nudist folks" wanted to speak with her. But *Senhora* Arminda was already prepared. In the background, I could hear her shouting: "They're a bunch of perverts! Tell him that I don't talk to scallywags!" a message that the maid transmitted with some difficulty: "scallywag" apparently was not a common term in her vocabulary. Struggling against the urge to slam down the phone, I insisted, and finally *Senhora* Arminda agreed to talk to Adamastor. But only by phone.

"I don't want that filthy man to set foot in my house."

Considering the hostile reception, Adamastor actually fared quite well. He explained that the play, based on the Bible, was not meant to scandalize anyone; they simply wanted to depict Paradise, as an allusion to Eden-Brazil itself. But *Senhora* Arminda was unshakeable: either you put an end to that sinful spectacle or I'll ruin your business. On the extension, I heard everything. It made me want to tell the women to go to hell; but I managed to contain myself. As for Adamastor, he was sad and bitter. All he wanted was to create a place where people could rediscover nature.

Just then, Gutiérrez showed up. He looked at us, surprised.

"What happened? You all look like you've been to a funeral. Who died?"

Paulo told him what had happened. To our surprise, Gutiérrez started to laugh. He laughed loudly; he laughed so hard that tears ran down his face while we looked at him, confused. Finally, he was able to control himself.

"Excuse me," he said, still gasping. "But that's hilarious. Hilarious."

"I don't see anything funny about it," said Adamastor, dryly. "What I see is trouble. Those fanatical women are going to drive us mad."

"Or they'll make us rich," retorted Gutiérrez.

"How?" Adamastor didn't understand. "You think that with those lunatics passing out flyers and blocking the road visitors are going to show up?"

"That's precisely why they'll show up," Gutiérrez guaranteed. "Don't you know that people love controversy and clamor? This is free publicity for us, Adamastor. You should even thank those old ladies from the League for the Defense of Morals. They are unwittingly helping Eden-Brazil. I don't think they'll give up either; they'll continue their campaign. Which will be great. Because the public will show up in throngs, you better believe it. I know what I'm talking about. I have experience with these sorts of things."

The first part of the prediction came true; the second didn't. The league's campaign continued, with furious enthusiasm. But the number of visitors didn't grow. To the contrary. The hotel had just a third of the rooms occupied, if that. The mini shopping center was selling very little, and the man who held the concession notified us that he was giving up on the business. The weather didn't help either: it was an exceptionally rainy year in Santa Catarina. Nobody wanted to go to the beach, even if it was in a paradisiacal location.

In short, putting up with this succession of misfortunes demanded a great deal of patience. As if this weren't enough, we also had to deal with a grotesque—and extremely unpleasant—incident. Involving Macedo.

During the time that he lived with us, nearly six months, Macedo had always behaved bizarrely. He did his job well; in fact, his ability to operate the serpent was simply stunning. After the shows, he would stay up for hours playing with it. He made it climb trees, slither around the house, and even dance to music. It made us laugh a lot. But he didn't do it to entertain us; to the contrary, he became irritated, offended by our comments. Then he would grab the snake and lock himself away in his room, from which then came the voice of Dóris Souza, making its case for sinfulness.

Paulo, always generous in spirit, tried to get Macedo to join the group, inviting him to meetings. Macedo would come, but he didn't participate at all; he didn't talk, he responded to questions with monosyllables.

But the situation changed when Isabel was there. Something would happen: Macedo would stare at her, with a look of adoration, drinking in her every word. An apparently platonic love, Paulo would say. Perfectly understandable, from my point of view. After all, she was a beautiful girl, and seeing her naked every day certainly must have messed with the guy a bit. I talked about this, in a joking way, with Paulo—but not with Adamastor, of course. At that point, I still had not been able to decipher the mysterious nature of his relationship with the girl. There was not the slightest evidence of a connection between the two of them; in the morning, for example, when we were getting up, the two of them would always emerge from their separate rooms. Logically, they could have been spending their nights together; but if so, why keep it a secret? Adamastor was a free man, unencumbered, as was the girl. Maybe he didn't want to mix business and pleasure, I sometimes thought, but that didn't make much sense either. After all, a relationship between the two of them would by no means negatively impact the project. I really wanted to ask Adamastor; our friendship would have made it possible. But I somehow knew that it was a taboo subject for him.

We were wrong, Paulo and I. Macedo's passion for Isabel wasn't platonic. Or, more precisely, suddenly it was no longer platonic.

One night I was awakened with a start by a noise in the hallway. A flurry of steps and then an irate voice—Isabel's—screaming at someone I couldn't identify. You didn't have to be a genius to figure out that someone had tried to get into her room and was repelled. But who? Most certainly, Adamastor. They had fought about something, and Isabel kicked him out. Despite my curiosity, I didn't get out of bed. I waited until morning to find out what had happened. I even thought about joking with Adamastor: so, finally we've found out your secret.

But the following morning held a surprise for me. The frustrated invader of Isabel's room was none other than Macedo, timid, strange Macedo. That was what Isabel herself told us at the breakfast table, told me, Paulo, and Adamastor. In the middle of the night, taking advantage of the fact that her door wasn't locked, the guy had snuck into her room.

"I turned on the light and there he was, right in front of me, naked, completely naked, trying to get into my bed. I told him to get out. He didn't even hear me, he was in his own world, and he tried to grab me. 'I love you, Isabel, I love you, without you life means nothing,' you know the line, right? It was really difficult to free myself from him."

She didn't seem indignant, to the contrary: she was laughing as she told the story (evidently she had some experience repelling intruders). Paulo and I also laughed, in the hopes of minimizing the weight of the incident—even to protect poor Macedo, who evidently was nothing more than a disturbed boy. Adamastor, however, was fuming. I had never seen him so angry.

"I'm going to teach that bastard a lesson," he said, "a lesson he'll never forget."

He leapt to his feet, and went to the guy's room. He came back, irritated.

"It's empty. But he must still be around. He didn't take his stuff."

"He probably hid in the jungle," said Paulo.

Which was likely—and would make finding him difficult. We

took off down the trail, Adamastor shouting: "I know you're there, Macedo! It's no use hiding! I'm going to beat the hell out of you, you idiot!"

Paulo and I, more used to these sorts of incidents, tried to calm him down: Macedo was nothing but a pitiful kid, incapable of controlling himself. Moreover, pervert or not, the fact was he was vital to our show; after all, nobody else knew how to control the serpent.

"I'll talk to him," said Paulo, the conciliator. "I guarantee he won't bother Isabel again. By now I'm sure he's aware of what a stupid thing he's done."

Still fuming, Adamastor agreed to head back. He wouldn't fire Macedo, but he also didn't want anything more to do with him; Paulo and I would have to deal with him. And he returned to the house.

Paulo and I continued the search. Our idea was to convince Macedo to apologize to Isabel and to Adamastor. We thought that this would put an end to the incident. But we couldn't find the kid. We walked for hours through the jungle, we even went down to the beach—nothing. This left us worried. It started to rain, and thus the day's performance would be cancelled, but what would we do if Macedo really had disappeared for good?

That night, Adamastor was awakened by a strange noise. He turned on the light and then had a terrible fright: there, at the foot of the bed, was the snake, curled up like it was just about to strike. Awakened by his shouts, Paulo and I ran to his room. And there we found the serpent. This was a mystery. Normally it was kept in the house, but locked up in the office. How did it get there? Adamastor had no doubts as to the answer.

"It was that lunatic Macedo. He must have operated the snake by remote control, from somewhere outside of the house."

He was furious. I tried to calm him down. I suggested that it could have been accidental: some short circuit had caused the snake to start moving on its own. Adamastor wasn't persuaded.

"An accident? And was it accidental that the snake came into my room and not yours? And how did it get in? Turning the doorknob with its coils, naturally."

"Maybe you left the door open?" Paulo offered.

"No way. This was planned, Paulo. The guy did this to threaten me. What he's saying is that he can get into my room. And kill me. But I'm going to get even with him, believe me. If he shows up around here again, you'll see."

Macedo didn't show up. The man in charge of the main entrance said that he had seen him, early that morning, with a suitcase, hitching a ride on the side of the road. That is, the guy had taken off.

"Not soon enough," grumbled Adamastor. "I don't need that pervert around."

This was not exactly the case. We soon figured out that none of us knew how to operate the snake. We fiddled with the controls but were only able to get stiff, grotesque movements out of it. And clips of its speech were repeated ten, fifteen times, like an old, vinyl record that was scratched. Moreover, its jaws remained closed at the moment when Eve—Isabel—was supposed to take the apple from them. Not even Jehovah could have opened it.

Adamastor consulted with a number of specialists in electronics. Useless. None of them could figure out how to fix the snake. We discussed the problem for a long time and arrived at the conclusion that we would have to do the scene with the snake immobilized, curled around a tree. One of Adamastor's employees would read the text of the animal's speech. After a number of attempts, we were able to put the damned snake in a suitable position—but by then the plastic that covered it had split in a few spots, revealing the internal mechanics, a problem we tried to fix with electrical tape. Even worse, Lucifer, Adamastor's monkey, now fearlessly played with the snake. That is, it no longer looked convincing to anyone.

That was just one of the problems. The other was the boycott by the League for the Defense of Morals, which went on gaining intensity. Once again, Adamastor made a decision: Isabel and I should cover our so-called private parts. Both Paulo and Gutiérrez were upset with the solution. Paulo thought that it was cowardice. Gutiérrez complained that the project was being disfigured.

"Disfigured or not, I don't care," Adamastor responded. "I have bills to pay, and I need visitors. And if there's anyone around here who can complain about their project being disfigured, it's me."

They asked my opinion, but, frankly, I didn't know what to say; the truth is I was still feeling a bit burned by the experience with *Hamlet in Brasília.*

"Either way is fine with me," said Isabel, who seemed to have lost interest not only in the play, but in Eden-Brazil as a whole. Which seemed to me a bad sign.

A seamstress put together for us a loincloth and a bikini that were designed to look like they were made out of fig leaves. Isabel's bikini didn't fit very well, and my loincloth looked ridiculous, but we carried on.

The results were, again, disastrous. The audience, ever smaller, complained: they had heard talk of a naked woman, and Isabel showed up in a bikini. What kind of a rip-off was this? On the other hand, the League for the Defense of Morals was still not satisfied. "Disguised nudity is still nudity," they now proclaimed in their flyers.

By that point, the project had been operating for about eight months—and it was still in the red. Adamastor was forced to let some employees go, and they immediately went to the labor courts to demand severance pay. And the problems continued to mount, appearing when least expected.

One day, Adamastor's ex-wife came to visit, accompanied by their son. Adamastor tried to treat them as well as possible, with our help. I even offered to give a tour of the place to the spoiled-brat son, who turned down the invitation: Disney World was a lot better. As for the ex-wife, she wasn't disposed toward our congeniality either. With a sour expression on her face, she criticized everything she saw. Finally, and during lunch—a lunch specially prepared by Adamastor himself, who had really outdone himself with the menu—she asked the question that revealed the true motives for her visit: is this thing turning a profit or not?

Adamastor said that it wasn't; the investment still hadn't shown a return. She had her doubts, and he said he would show her the books. The woman went into a rage. She got up, shouting: this whole thing was a joke, the product of depraved minds, Adamastor was throwing away money that, by law, belonged to her and their son. Dragging Herodotus, who was also complaining (but about not having gotten to swim in the ocean), she got into the taxi that was waiting and took off.

We remained there, in silence. I tried to come up with something optimistic to say.

"It's better this way, Adamastor. She won't bother you again."

"That's what you think," he said, bitterly. "The first thing she's going to do is talk to a lawyer. She'll want to get her hands on this before it's over."

And that's what happened: two days later a fax arrived from a *Senhor* Arnóbio. He said that he was Elisa's lawyer and that he was requesting clarification regarding the legal situation of the property, the amounts invested into it, profits, etc. This seemed a sign of great tribulations to come. And the trials of poor Adamastor had not reached an end. He was to receive still yet another unexpected visit.

One morning, I was having breakfast, still half asleep, when, looking out the window, I noticed some sort of tent set up in front of the house. A precarious tent, made of black plastic. Who could be inside of it? Had Adamastor hired another worker and housed him this way? But Adamastor hadn't mentioned anything to me. Moreover, there wasn't any more money for that.

I went to his room. He was sitting up in bed, perfectly still, lost in his thoughts, something that had been happening a lot lately. I asked him about the tent. He didn't know anything about it.

"Tent?" he asked, surprised. "What tent? It's news to me."

He jumped out of bed, put on his shorts, and the two of us went to check it out. The tent had one of its ends open, and through it we could see someone lying down. A grimy foot was sticking out. A foot that Adamastor poked.

"What's going on, buddy? What are you doing here?"

A man emerged from the tent. He was the same age as Adamastor, but he was, you could see, in ruins: skinny, bent over, a patchy beard. He was dressed in rags, and the smell that emanated from him was intolerable. Seeing Adamastor, he smiled, revealing a few broken teeth.

"Don't you recognize me, comrade Adamastor?"

Adamastor's jaw dropped. He was stunned.

"Marcelo! Is that you, man?"

Marcelo: I had heard about him. Adamastor had told me the story of his classmate. The question was, What had happened to the guy? That was the question Adamastor asked, and that Marcelo preferred not to answer. Never mind, he said, I'll tell you some other time.

"And how did you find me here?"

He smiled, toothlessly and mysteriously.

"I have my sources, Adamastor. Do you remember when we used to talk about the political struggle? You remember how much I emphasized the importance of information? Well, I'm here thanks to some information I received. Some information about your project. Eden-Brazil. And that's why I'm here, Adamastor. My mission here is political."

He stopped speaking. Adamastor was so surprised he couldn't say anything.

"Don't you want to know what this mission is?" Marcelo asked. And, since the still astonished Adamastor didn't respond, he continued:

"In that case, I'll tell you. We lost touch with each other years ago, Adamastor, so you likely aren't aware that I'm part of the Landless Movement. Do you remember how we talked about the importance of agrarian reform? Well, I decided to put my ideas into practice. This country is feudal, Adamastor. Enormous tracts of land are concentrated in the hands of the very few. You know this; I explained it to you a number of times. Now, these landlords aren't going to turn over their lands out of the goodness of their hearts. It will only happen under pressure. And that's my role: to identify underutilized properties. I'm a sort of vanguard of the movement. I'm the first to arrive, the first to occupy. Then I notify my comrades. They come by the hundreds, by the thousands. And then . . ."

"Wait a second," Adamastor interrupted, panicked. "Are you telling me my property is going to be occupied?"

"That's exactly what I'm telling you, Adamastor. I've never seen such an underutilized landholding. You might fool others with this story about a nature reserve, this Eden-Brazil. You don't fool me. I've already explored the place and confirmed: you don't have anything of value here. There's not even one bean plant planted. The area is what it's been for the last thousand years. In fact, the only thing different I saw was some sort of stuffed snake hanging from a tree . . ." He laughed. "I guess that must be to try to frighten off activists like me. But it didn't work, Adamastor. I'm not afraid of guns, much less fake animals."

I stared at the man. Mostly because of his teeth, which fascinated and repulsed me. In the back of his mouth he had a few teeth remaining, but in the bottom front there was one single, giant, decaying tooth. Like a tower that, though partially destroyed, still resisted, standing among a razed city. It told a story, that tooth. And it was also a symbol.

Dental evaluations aside, I was worried. Really worried. The guy seemed crazy to me, but if what he was saying was true, we were facing a big headache down the road. Technically, the property was underutilized; the Landless would have a go of it here. But this Marcelo went on.

"Now there is a potential solution. In some special cases—and your case, Adamastor, has something special about it: you're moved by some ideal, this environmentalism thing, and, moreover, you're my friend—we can negotiate. We're in need of money, Adamastor, just as much as we're in need of land. If you make a decent donation, I can convince folks to occupy somebody else's land."

He looked at him. "What do you say?"

"And how much would this donation need to be?" Adamastor asked, and his worry was more than apparent.

The other guy mentioned a figure. Not very big, but also not very small.

"I don't think I have that kind of money," said Adamastor, in a voice that betrayed his insecurity.

"Come up with it then," said Marcelo. "If it takes a little while, that's alright. I can spend two or three days here in this tent, as long as you make arrangements for food, of course, and you let me use your bathroom. We, the Landless, are used to waiting. For centuries we've been waiting for justice to be done. We can wait a bit longer. But tell me, how's your life been? And how's your project going?"

Though a bit hesitant, Adamastor began to speak. I continued to watch the guy, who now smiled, satisfied.

An idea occurred to me. I excused myself and went into the house. Ten minutes later, I came back.

"I have some news for you, Adamastor," I said. "You don't need to donate a dime."

"What?" said Adamastor, surprised. A surprise that was certainly shared by his toothless friend, if in a different way: with some alarm.

"It's just that I had some doubts, you know. Some doubts about our friend here. So I decided to telephone the directorate of the Landless Movement—I have a friend there, a good friend, a guy I can trust. And this friend of mine said that there's no Marcelo in the movement. And that they're not planning to occupy any properties at this time."

Marcelo's first reaction was one of fear—the fear of someone who has been caught red-handed. But he quickly composed himself. He smiled, confidently.

"Of course that's what he had to tell you. As I said, my work is done in secret. They have instructions to deny that they know me. They're not going to turn in one of their agents, are they? Huh? What do you think?"

He stared at us, and his gaze was like that of a cornered animal. Adamastor and I were silent. And then Marcelo fell to his knees, sobbing.

"I'm worthless, Adamastor, I'm nothing but trash, I don't even know how to lie—oh, I'm so ashamed, Adamastor, I'm so ashamed . . ."

Adamastor embraced him. For an instant the two of them remained like that, hugging one another, Marcelo crying. Finally he was able to control himself. Sniffling, he began to take down the tent. Suddenly he stopped.

"There's something I want to ask of you, Adamastor, just one thing. I want some dentures. For years, I haven't known what it's like to properly chew food . . . There's a dentist who will give me a really good deal on a set of dentures. Will you help me?"

Without a word, Adamastor took what money he had in his pocket and handed it to the man, who looked at him with adoration.

"Thank you, Adamastor. Thank you so much. You are a better man than I am, comrade. It's not hard to be better than me—but, well, you are a much, much better man than I am."

"You can leave the tarp here if you want," said Adamastor.

Marcelo looked at him, and there was a fierce irony in his gaze.

"And where am I going to live?" he asked. "Even on occupied land we need to shelter ourselves, Adamastor."

The black plastic rolled up under his arm, he left. Adamastor and I remained there for a while, watching the outline of him disappear into the distance.

"You believed his story?" I asked.

"I don't know," sighed Adamastor. "Frankly, I don't know. I think I wanted to believe it. That guy used to mean a lot to me, Richie. He was my guru, my role model, the guy I wanted to emulate. How could I not believe him? It was your telephone call that changed everything."

"I didn't make a call."

"What?" He was shocked. "So you invented the whole conversation?"

"Don't forget I'm an actor, my friend. A bad actor, but an actor nonetheless. I learned how to create situations that in reality don't exist. Yes, I lied. I lied just like he was lying. But I know how to lie better than he does, Adamastor."

And I added, sarcastically, "Maybe I need to use this talent a bit more often."

By which I was being entirely prophetic.

8

THE END OF THE DREAM?

With the number of visitors shrinking and debts mounting, the people who worked at Eden-Brazil started to disappear. The hotel and the shopping center had to be closed. Paulo, whose paycheck was late, went to see Adamastor. With a great deal of tact, as was his manner, he alleged that the play no longer needed a director, that his presence at Eden-Brazil was no longer necessary. Adamastor quickly understood. An amount was negotiated, Paulo took it and left. With a great deal of sadness, I said goodbye to him. Unlike Nelson from *Hamlet in Brasília*, he was a decent guy, a friend through good times and bad.

Isabel and I continued to put on our show for the ever-smaller audiences—there was one day when the only person was a fat old woman who came out from behind the bamboo to boo and insult us.

"You clowns! You're not worth the ticket price!"

I responded in kind, with every piece of profanity that I knew, but Isabel seemed indifferent. Which confirmed my suspicions. She no longer cared the least bit about Eden-Brazil; she gave the impression she was doing us all a favor. And, one interesting detail, she almost always spent the night away. Where? With whom?

This obviously irritated Adamastor, but I didn't dare ask him about it. With the crises, he had begun to confide in me—in truth, I was the only one he seemed to be able to trust. Even so, he didn't talk about Isabel, though the situation with his niece, or supposed niece, worried him.

One day Gutiérrez paid us a visit. It had been some time since he'd come by. For me, his absence was surprising—after all, he halfway considered himself responsible for the idea of the project—but not for Adamastor, who would say, bitterly: He's the type of guy who disappears as soon as things start to go badly. But Gutiérrez came, well dressed, as always, and effusive, as always. We were having dinner, Adamastor and I. I took the initiative of inviting him to sit down and join us for what little food there was, but he refused, explaining that he had an appointment and was just passing by. After some pleasantries—it sure has been hot, that sort of thing—he announced, in a completely casual tone:

"By the way, Adamastor, I think it's time for us to end our partnership. Unfortunately, the project didn't work, and I can't waste more time here. You know how valuable my time is. Anyways, I'm moving to Mexico, and I'm going to start a business venture there.

He cleared his throat and added: "And Isabel is going with me."

Ah, yes, now it was clear: this guy was the reason for Isabel's mysterious disappearances. She was having an affair with Gutiérrez. And cheating on Adamastor.

I looked at Adamastor. As incredible as it seems, he maintained complete control of himself. His face, stony, did not reveal the slightest emotion: not anger, not disgust, not anguish, nothing. He remained completely motionless, silent. This got to Gutiérrez. He quickly lost all of his arrogance, all his supposed self-confidence.

"I know this must seem like a tremendous betrayal," he said, in a hesitant voice. "But believe me, Adamastor, it's nothing personal. Isabel and I fell in love, that's what happened. We didn't want to tell you before because she wasn't sure if she really wanted to live with me. Now she's decided, and we're leaving together. Because there's nothing more to do here. Adamastor. Eden-Brazil was a great idea, it could have been a success, but these people didn't understand the project. This is something for the First World, not for these provincials. You have two alternatives: either sell all this for the best price you can get and leave, or . . ."

He hesitated for an instant, then he took a piece of paper out of his pocket. It was cut out of a newspaper.

"This here," he explained, "gave me an idea, one last idea for Eden-Brazil. It's a bit desperate, but, if done well, could result in a decent payoff. If you want, I'll explain it to you. It's the last bit of help I can offer."

Adamastor remained silent, impassive. Gutiérrez sighed.

"I can see you don't want to talk to me. I understand completely, Adamastor. I only ask that you forgive me, me and Isabel. Well, I'm off. I'm going to leave this article here. Read it. If you come up with the same idea I did, go for it."

He put the clipping on the table and left.

The two of us stayed there. In silence. Adamastor remained completely still, in the same position. A fly crawled across his forehead, but he didn't brush it off. What was he thinking? I had no idea? But I could imagine his anguish. At that moment, he had reached bottom. After the failure of his project, his business consultant—some consultant, that guy—was abandoning him, and worse, he was leaving with Isabel. What type of relationship had they had, she and Adamastor, remained a mystery to me; but surely the fact that Gutiérrez was taking her away represented a betrayal. About this Adamastor would say nothing. He got up and, without a word, went to his room.

The next day was really heavy. In many senses. In the first place, the sky was dark with clouds, and the heat meant that it was going to rain. In addition, Adamastor was still mute. He said good morning, of course, but he had breakfast in silence—a breakfast that I myself had prepared: at that point we no longer had a maid. The only person who continued working for Eden-Brazil was the old guy who kept watch at the main entrance. After we finished, Adamastor said that he was going for a walk.

"Would you like me to come along?"

He said no, he preferred to be alone. And, in fact, he only showed up again that night. We sat down to dinner, but he ate almost nothing. I took his plate to the sink, and then we sat there in silence. A silence only occasionally interrupted by a distant thunder. I didn't know what to do. He responded to my questions only with monosyllables, which only served to heighten my anxiety.

The newspaper clipping Gutiérrez had brought was still there on the table. I picked it up and began to read.

"Swedish foundation wants to protect native Brazilians," was the title of the article, which announced the arrival in São Paulo of the representative from a Swedish foundation dedicated to protecting cultures in danger of extinction, such as indigenous cultures. In an interview, the representative—Professor Gunnar Magnusson—said that projects to assist these cultures could receive substantial financial support. The article ended with a contact number.

Why had Gutiérrez cut out this article? And why did he say that it could lead to some money? The foundation was offering support, but I didn't see how we could qualify for it. Yes, Adamastor had conceived of Eden-Brazil as a place for the preservation of the environment; it even contained expanses of the Atlantic Forest. But it seemed the Swedes weren't interested in the Atlantic Forest, they were interested in Indians. And we didn't have Indians.

And then Adamastor broke his silence. Without looking at me, in a slightly hoarse, almost inaudible voice, he said, "I owe you an apology, Richie. I invited you to come here, I made you promises, and now everything has failed."

I started to protest, to say that's the life of an actor, one day you're up, and the next day you're down, or vice versa, but he cut me off with a gesture.

"Don't try to minimize things, Richie. Our situation is extremely bad, you know that."

A pause, then he continued.

"If you want to go, feel free to do so. I can arrange for some money for you, not much, but enough for you to restart your life elsewhere."

I laughed. A forced laugh, but a laugh nonetheless.

"Don't go there, Adamastor. I've enjoyed all this, and as long as you stay, I'll stay too. You won't get rid of me so easily."

He smiled. A faint smile.

"Thank you, buddy. The first time I saw you, I was sure of one thing: you not only have talent, you have character."

He sighed.

"It's just that now our problem isn't character, it's money."

He looked at his watch.

"It's late. I think I'm going to bed. We'll talk tomorrow."

He got up and went to his room. I sat on the veranda, looking at the rain now falling. Lightning flashes lit up the sea and the dark jungle on the side of the mountain. It was beautiful, really beautiful. After the rain stopped, the clouds broke up, and an enormous moon appeared.

9

ENORMOUS MOON IN THE SKY—
SMALL LIGHT AT THE END
OF THE TUNNEL

I stayed there thinking for a good while. About what? My life, first of all. Mom was right to be disgusted with me. There I was, twenty years old, without a job, without a career, without anything. My last hope, the play for Eden-Brazil, had turned out to be a flop. What to do now? Return home with my tail between my legs? I didn't much like that idea. In part because I didn't want to abandon Adamastor. The truth is he had trusted me to help him turn his dream into reality. That dream was now done for, but I didn't want to be like one of those rats fleeing a sinking ship. Furthermore, the poor guy was so down, so depressed, that there was a risk he might do something stupid. No, he needed friends. And the only friend available was me.

While I ruminated over these thoughts, I realized I was still holding the newspaper article in my hand. I read it again in the moonlight, and again I was intrigued. What was there that could result in the "decent payoff" that Gutiérrez had mentioned. Indians—but where were we going to come up with Indians? And Indians from endangered tribes?

Suddenly I understood.

Gutiérrez wasn't talking about real Indians. He was talking about a performance like what we had put together. That is, actors playing the role of Indians. What he was saying was this: invent some Indians here, say that they are the last descendants of an endangered tribe, and ask for money from the Swedes to help the poor fellows.

A risky proposition. We would have to fool this Magnusson guy. Still worse, we would have to recruit people. And who could assure us they would be people we could trust? We already had Marcelo as precedent. Were we once again going to have to deal with that sort of complication? Only Gutiérrez would come up with an idea like this. The only thing that could have made it more outlandish would be if he had proposed android Indians. I was just about to tear up the article, irritated, when suddenly a question came to mind: why would there need to be Indians, in the plural? Why not just one Indian, the only survivor from a legendary tribe?

A not completely groundless hypothesis. I had read about many indigenous cultures that now were reduced to half a dozen people, including there in Santa Catarina. A single Indian would be even more dramatic. And it would justify, for that foundation, a dedication of funds.

Now, who would be the Indian?

Me.

Who else? Me, of course. The guy who had played the part of Adam could quite well play the part of a native Brazilian. Moreover, my physical type would help. With a bit of rehearsal, I would become José de Alencar's Peri.

I took a deep breath. My God, this was a real challenge. Playing a role like this was like nothing I'd ever done. And it wasn't just a challenge, it was a transgression. After all, we would be defrauding foreigners. Something that could lead to jail time, maybe even a diplomatic incident. On the other hand, if we didn't come up with some money, Adamastor would soon wind up in court because of his debts—and because of his ex-wife. We were caught between the fire and the frying pan. Now, for me, what was really tempting was the challenge. The challenge of inhabiting a character without a name, who didn't exist in any script, who wasn't even present—beyond an imprecise, undefined shadow—in my own imagination. That is, I would have to create him practically out of nothing.

I leapt to my feet as if propelled by a spring, I looked at the moon, fearless.

"Yes!" I shouted. "I'll do it!"

I would do it. But first I had to tell Eden-Brazil's owner.

I went to Adamastor's room. The door was open, so I went in. I turned on the light. There he was, sleeping. A restless sleep: he shifted around, mumbling unintelligibly. Cautiously, I nudged him.

"Wake up, Adamastor. Wake up!"

He sat up, eyes wide open, a frightened expression on his face.

"The snake? Is it the snake again?"

The poor guy was confused. It seems the word "snake," or anything that sounded like snake, like the word "wake," that I naturally had used, was associated in his mind with the night that he woke up with the electronic serpent in his bedroom. It was funny, but also pathetic.

"No, Adamastor. It's not a snake. It's me, Richie. You remember me? The Adam of Eden-Brazil."

He smiled, a bit embarrassed. Then he frowned: what was I thinking, waking him up in the middle of the night?

"You know perfectly well I've been having insomnia because of all this stress," he complained. "I'm finally able to get to sleep, and you come and wake me up. That's cruel, Richie. Really cruel. I don't deserve this, do I? Turn off the light and get out of here. We'll talk in the morning."

He turned to lie down, covering himself with the sheet. I didn't give up.

"No, Adamastor. Forgive me, but it's important. An idea came to me, one that might save us. That's what I want to talk to you about. Now."

He threw aside the sheet and sat up on the side of the bed.

"You're a real pain in the neck, aren't you? Okay, tell me what you have to say. Tell me this marvelous idea you had in the middle of the night."

I showed him the article. He looked at me, irritated.

"Again, that thing? I'm not interested."

He laid down again and again covered himself with the sheet. I tore the sheet off him.

"Listen, Adamastor, you have to hear me out. This article could be Eden-Brazil's salvation. It could be your salvation."

He looked at me, intrigued.

"What do you mean? What are you talking about?"

I explained to him my idea. As I expected, he didn't seem at all enthused. Quite the opposite.

"No way, man. I won't get in involved in something like that. I might be a dreamer, I might be naïve, but a con man I am not."

Okay, that was the same reservation that I had with the plan too. But then I tried to convince him, and myself. In fact, we would be, as the saying goes, writing straight with crooked lines.

"There are so many corrupt people out there, Adamastor. There are guys stealing public funds, there are guys running cons in the street. That's not what we're going to do. We're going to develop an environmental project—is there anything else more deserving? The Europeans and the Americans always accuse

Brazilians of destroying forests. Not us: we are preserving them. Not only that, we are going to teach people to care for nature, just like you wanted. It's true that those guys' money isn't exactly for this purpose, but what difference does it make? If there aren't any Indians around here, it's not our fault. And if they did exist, you most certainly would take care of them. At least for your intentions, you deserve support."

Adamastor stroked his goatee. I already knew him well enough to know that this meant he was halfway to yes: he was no longer rejecting the proposal. He asked how we would pull this off, in practical terms.

10

THE DESCENDANT OF PERI

Well, for that I had an answer: the Indian would be me. A timid, fleeting Indian. The only survivor of a family—maybe from the Xokleng, Indians that had been removed from their lands by the building of a dam—I would stay in the jungle.

"But this means," Adamastor pondered, "that you'll have to spend your days in the jungle. Maybe many days. That won't be easy."

"True. But our situation isn't easy either. What's more, if the Indians can survive in the jungle, why can't I? Don't forget, my father was an Indian . . ."

He laughed. He thought about it for a bit and then raised another question.

"You said you would play the part of an Indian who remains hidden. But if you stay hidden, how is the Swede going to know that you exist?"

"Don't worry. I'll come up with a way to be spotted by him, even if just for a second."

"And if the guy wants to see you up close? If he wants to record your voice, for example? After all, you'll be the only one left who speaks a language in extinction."

"But you won't allow that to happen. You will allege that it's dangerous, not for him, but for me: Indians are at risk of contracting the diseases of white men."

He was silent for a moment. Then he made a dismissive gesture.

"I don't know, man. I don't know. This seems pretty crazy."

"So what, Adamastor? At this point we have to give anything a shot. Even if it seems crazy."

He sighed. "Okay. Let's do it. It's in God's hands now." He laughed. "Or, better, it's in *Tupã*'s hands now."

We decided that the following day we would call the person representing the foundation in Brazil. And then we went to bed. But I was so excited, I couldn't sleep. I tossed and turned in bed. When I finally was able to fall asleep, I had strange dreams: Indians, snakes, and Lucifer, the monkey . . . I woke up sweating, but I preferred to attribute that to the heat.

After breakfast, Adamastor made the call. I listened in on the other line. A woman's voice answered, warm and polite, someone who identified herself as Sílvia Campos, assistant to the representative of the foundation. I'm calling about the article in the newspaper, said Adamastor, and he told the story, just as we had agreed upon—and with a degree of confidence that surprised me; it seemed he had gotten into the spirit of things sooner than I could have imagined.

Sílvia was interested. She excused herself, spoke with someone in a language we didn't recognize—Swedish, most certainly—and then said that she and the representative were traveling to Rio Grande do Sul, where they would visit indigenous communities. On the way, they could make a stop in Santa Catarina to learn about our reserve. This would be in two days. She asked for a formal invitation to be faxed to them.

I confess that I felt a chill come over me. Of course at some point the plan would have to be put to the test; but I didn't imagine that this would happen within forty-eight hours. It was better this way though: a long wait would be unnerving—and unnecessary: not much preparation was needed for my performance. So as soon as Sílvia Campos hung up the phone I said to Adamastor that we needed to outline the plan.

First question: how could I inhabit the role of the Indian? Clothing was out of the question: it wasn't likely that the foundation would help an acculturated Indian; they most certainly would prefer an authentic one, like those that the Portuguese met when they first arrived in Brazil. That is, nude. And I didn't want to be naked. I had become a bit traumatized by nudity. I would use a loincloth—made of what? We discussed it a bit, and we opted for an old piece of buckskin, a bit moth-eaten, that Adamastor had found in the basement of the house. It seems that deer had once been common in the region, so this sort of dress was appropriate. One question emerged: should I paint myself with annatto or some other natural coloring? In school I had learned that the Indians made use of that sort of thing, but it had to do with tribal customs. A solitary Indian, alone in the forest, wouldn't have anyone for whom to paint himself. Maybe he would just be dirty all the time. Perfect: dirt would be part of the costume. And it would also demonstrate the need for care for the poor native.

One question the Swede and his assistant would certainly ask was, Why did the Indian stay there, in a place that had nearly become a theme park?

Adamastor made up a story. Peri (this was the code name we assigned to this imaginary character, and to the entire plan, Operation Peri) avoided white men, but apparently he trusted

Adamastor. And why did he trust Adamastor? Answer: Adamastor respected him, he didn't try to bring him into the so-called civilized world. He also left food for him, which the Indian never refused. If he ever became ill, Adamastor would be able to provide care for the Indian, who would not reject his help.

As we came up with answers to the many questions, Adamastor grew increasingly enthusiastic. By the end, he was nearly euphoric.

"I think it's going to work, Richie. As incredible as it seems, I think it's going to work. I can already see you as Peri."

I couldn't. I still couldn't see myself as Peri. It's one thing to perform a role for two hours on stage; it's another to inhabit a character for days (how many days was unknown; it would depend on the Swede's interest). The truth is, I was always a city kid. Now I would have to transform myself into a creature of the jungle. I would have to give up the comforts of a house, a bed, a bathroom. Sleeping on the ground, relieving myself in the brush—was I going to be able to deal with all that?

I didn't talk to Adamastor about my doubts—but he soon sensed them: at that point we were close enough for that to be possible. He tried to reassure me; after all, I wouldn't be completely on my own. If anything happened, he would be nearby, I just had to let him know. He suggested that I take with me cans of food and other provisions that I could hide someplace far from the house. I could also keep a tarp, in case of strong rain, which was frequent at that time of year. And also Adamastor's powerful binoculars; from far away I could follow what was happening at the house.

"I'm going to want a cell phone," I told him. "So we can stay in contact."

He laughed.

"An Indian using a cell phone? I've never heard of such a thing.

I think you're going to have to communicate with smoke signals. Just kidding, buddy, just kidding. We have to get into the spirit of things."

The spirit of it was different from the thing itself, as I found out the next day—a day I spent exploring the jungle. And I soon figured out that it would be much worse than I had imagined. I wasn't used to walking barefoot, for example. And the bugs—my God, there were so many bugs there! In the clearing where we had performed the play this wasn't a problem. But in the middle of the jungle it was hell. I was bitten about a hundred times, and soon I was covered in welts that itched like the devil. But, if the Indians could tolerate it, I would have to as well.

The sacrifice, however, came with some compensation: the ties of friendship between Adamastor and me had strengthened a great deal. We were already friends, but now we had become—despite the difference in age—almost brothers. Until then he had been, above all, the owner of the property, the boss; he treated me well, but there was a certain distance between us. Now that distance had disappeared. He seemed very grateful for the effort I was putting in, and that's what he said to me, that night, as we were having dinner.

"You know, I've never had a lot of friends. As a matter of fact, I've never had much luck with relationships. My marriage was a failure, as you yourself saw. My wife hates me. With my son, there's no communication. With you, I'm discovering friendship. I'm very grateful to you for that."

He paused and then, without my having touched upon the subject, without my having asked him about it, he started to talk about Isabel. With great effort, of course; it was painful for him.

As I had suspected, she wasn't his niece. He met her in a bar where she worked, in Florianópolis. He had given her presents, expensive clothes, jewelry, had taken her to fancy restaurants.

But nothing had happened between the two of them, nothing. She manipulated him like a puppet. And then the Eden-Brazil project began.

"When she found out about the play, she got the idea that she had to come play the role of Eve: theater was what she dreamed of doing with her life. I agreed with everything. My hope was to win her love here. An illusion, man, pure illusion. In the end, she took off with that Gutiérrez."

A silence descended, a heavy, anguished silence. The telephone rang; it was Sílvia, letting us know they would be arriving the next day, as agreed upon. She asked if Adamastor could pick them up at the airport. Adamastor said yes, that he was at their disposal. He hung up and looked at me.

"They're really coming, Richie. Now it's all up to you. Or nearly all up to you."

I can admit now I felt a knot in the pit of my stomach, but I wasn't going to admit it then.

"Leave it to me, Adamastor. Operation Peri will be a success, you'll see."

He looked at his watch.

"I think we should get some sleep. Tomorrow we have to be sharp—for whatever may or may not happen."

A thought came to him, and he laughed.

"Try to appreciate your bed. We don't know when you'll next sleep in it."

11

THE NEW PRODUCTION BEGINS

The next day, I woke up early. I had breakfast and put on my loincloth. I looked at myself in the mirror. As an Indian, I wasn't very convincing. But I could change that. I said goodbye to Adamastor and went into the forest. The first thing I did was cover myself with mud; I also tied a piece of vine around my forehead, pulling back by hair, which at that time was long. Okay, Adam had given way to Peri. And then I took the binoculars and climbed up a tree—with some effort—to keep an eye on the house. I saw Adamastor drive away; I calculated that he would return in about three hours—the airport wasn't nearby. And in fact, just after noon the car returned. Adamastor got out, along with a very tall, somewhat ungainly looking blond man: the Swede. Oh yeah, and Sílvia. A beautiful girl. Not as beautiful as Isabel perhaps, but of a distinct sort of beauty, an aristocratic beauty: tall, blond, wearing an elegantly tailored suit . . . She wasn't made for just any Peri, this Sílvia.

From where they were, Adamastor pointed toward the jungle. I could imagine him saying, that's where the young Indian we spoke about lives, the last of his tribe. Both the Swede and Sílvia looked attentively. She served as interpreter for Magnusson, who probably was asking a lot of questions since they stayed there a long time talking. Finally, they went inside. They would stay at the house, which we had planned on and for which I had taken certain precautions, including locking the door to my room.

That night, Adamastor served them dinner. An elaborate dinner, I deduced from the number of serving trays. I, on the other hand, only had canned ham and an orange. Truth is, I wasn't hungry. I was too anxious to find out what they had discussed.

Close to midnight, the cell phone rang.

"Sorry I didn't call earlier," said Adamastor. "But I couldn't; they just went to bed. I've never met a more talkative pair . . . Were you sleeping?"

"Of course," I said, sarcastically. "Here in my king-sized bed with the silk canopy and satin sheets. What are you thinking, Adamastor? You think it's easy to get to sleep here?"

"No, no I don't. But I want to remind you this was your idea. You can't complain."

"I'm not complaining. I want to know what you talked about."

"The Swedish guy is very interested . . ."

"Does he speak Portuguese?"

"Not a word. The girl, Sílvia, interprets for him. She lived in Sweden for a long time and speaks the language fluently. And she's very smart. In fact, she's too smart, if you ask me."

"Why? Do you think she doesn't buy something about our story?"

"Maybe. She's Brazilian, you know what that means, she knows what sort of cons people are capable of in this country."

"And him?"

"Him, no. He not only bought it, he's excited about it. He said that a case like this would be a first. He even talked about children that had been lost in the forest and that had been raised by animals . . . In short, he wants to see you. That is, not you. He wants to see the Indian."

"And what did you say?"

"What we agreed on. That you—that is, the Indian—are very shy, that we only see you once in a while . . ."

"Did you tell them that I accept food? Not me, that is, the Indian."

"I did. And I said that we were able to take care of you here, and that if you got sick, for example, we could provide for a doctor. Not you, that is, the Indian. Peri. Well, what we know is they want to see you. They were going to stay for two days, but now they're willing to prolong their stay: a week, ten days, if necessary."

A week in the jungle. That was going to be hard. A week being bitten by insects, a week relieving myself in the bushes . . . I was hoping they would be content to hear the story and, having seen me once or twice, they would leave—leaving behind some funding, of course. I never imagined my performance, *The Last Indian of a Disappearing Tribe*, would be such a success.

I sighed.

"Okay, Adamastor. We'll carry on with the plan as agreed upon. If they're buying it, that's what's important."

He asked if I needed anything. I said no. He said goodnight and hung up.

I decided to look for a place to sleep. Fortunately, it wasn't raining, so I wouldn't need to set up the tent. But I thought about the mosquitoes and the animals—and I decided to wrap myself in the tarp. I took it to a clearing, gathered together some leaves—which would serve as a mattress—and I laid down.

But I couldn't get to sleep. Funny: I had slept in bus stations and on park benches. But there, drowsiness just wouldn't come to me.

Because of the jungle, of course. Because of the jungle sounds, the thousand sounds of the jungle and of the jungle animals, the cracks, the whistles, the buzzes, the chirps, the hisses. I covered my ears, but it didn't help. At that moment, I felt like the children who, in fairy tales, got lost in the forest. It's just that the jungle wasn't like your typical forest. Forests, like those I had seen in photos and paintings, were made up of those huge, majestic trees, oaks and sequoias. Not there. There we were dealing with thick, nearly impenetrable vegetation. The jungle was dense, dark, enigmatic. Like my father.

Oh, how I missed my father. I was just then starting to realize that: my father had told me stories, yes, stories about the Amazon jungle, and I liked those stories, but he never talked about himself, about his fears, his hopes, his aspirations. My father died before I had a chance to really know him. My father died before we had a chance to really have a conversation. An enormous sadness came over me, even making me forget my fear. Soon I was softly crying, calling out for my father and my mother, until I finally fell asleep.

As an Indian, I really wasn't any good at all, as I could tell when I woke up the next morning: the sun was already high up in the sky. At that hour, any Guarani worth his salt would already be out hunting, or fishing, or making war. There I was, bleary-eyed—and incredibly sore; despite the leaves, the ground was, inevitably, hard. With a groan, I got up. And, at that moment, I heard voices. Or, better: I heard a voice. It was Adamastor, speaking very loudly. And it wasn't hard to guess why he was speaking so loudly. He already knew me well enough to know that—as had happened—quite probably I would have overslept. So he was alerting me to his presence, and that of the Swede and Sílvia. In fact, peeking through the trees, I spotted them walking along what had in the original project been denominated an eco-trail.

Adamastor explained that via that trail, without disturbing the ecosystem, visitors could have an idea of the vitality of the Atlantic tropical forest.

"And it was around here," he added, "that we first spotted the Indian."

Was that a signal for me? Without a doubt. I quickly hid the tarp, applied a bit more mud on my face and body and ran to the spot where the trail came to an end, at the side of the mountain where the jungle became much denser. My idea was for them to see me through the trees. They would be able to see me but not pursue me. The Swede was no longer a young man, he walked with some difficulty, and the girl was too urbane to set off into the jungle. I was already in a fight against time because, though they began to walk more slowly, opening up a path through the jungle was more difficult. At one point I stubbed my toe on a fallen tree—and I even saw stars, the pain was so great. Still, I continued on, and about a hundred meters from the end of the trail I caught up with them. Staying within the jungle, I ran past them, trying to make as much noise as possible. It worked.

"There he is!" Adamastor shouted.

Sílvia looked around, evidently disappointed: she wasn't able to locate the Indian. But the enthusiastic shouts of the Swede showed that, at least for an instant, he had spotted me. But, as I expected, he decided not to follow me.

"Did you see?" Adamastor asked, triumphantly. "Did you see our Indian?"

Sílvia was now asking a bunch of questions—that I would have liked to hear, but I thought it prudent to keep moving away. Limping—my toe was hurting a lot—I returned to my hideout. I was famished, and the cell phone was there. It could ring at any moment with news from Adamastor about our first encounter.

I opened a tin of sardines. My idea was to eat them on bread, but the bread was covered with ants. So my meal—breakfast and lunch—was just that, sardines. It wasn't exactly a banquet, I can assure you. But I was so hungry that if there were nothing else I might have even eaten the tin itself.

An hour later, the cell phone rang. Adamastor was electric.

"Sensational! You were great, man! Absolutely convincing! If there were an Oscar for the best portrayal of an Indian, you would have won it!"

I contained my irritation and tried to return the compliment.

"You were great too. From what I could hear, you convinced the both of them."

"I did what I could," he responded, modestly. A pause, and he added: "But we're going to have to change our script a bit."

"Why?"

"Because they want to photograph you."

"Photograph me, but how, Adamastor? You don't want me to pose for them, with the expression of a poor, helpless Indian on my face . . ."

He laughed.

"No. But they said they need photos for the dossier that they will send to the president of the foundation. The awarding of a grant will depend on this dossier. Gunnar said assistance is assured, that I can already count on funding—but the procedures need to be followed. Have courage, Peri. It won't be hard. All you have to do is pass by the trail a bit more slowly. You're as fast as lightning, man. Moving like that, no camera could ever get a shot of you."

His proposal made sense. We agreed that the next day he would take them again on the eco-trail. Everything happened as planned, and when they had their cameras ready I passed by running—not very fast, which, by the way, I couldn't have done even if I wanted to: my foot was still hurting—and taking care not to show my face. It worked. They got a number of pictures of me, Gunnar barely able to contain his euphoria.

I thought that would be enough and that now they would leave. But, via the cell phone, Adamastor said that it wasn't.

"They decided to record a video showing the property. And I'm going to be in it, talking about you."

That meant another night or two in the jungle, more sardines, more ants, more stubbed toes. Fine: the plan was working, and that's what mattered. Little did I know what was going to happen.

12

GETTING–BY FORCE OF DESTINY–REAL

In the morning, I woke up feeling a bit woozy, with a headache, and not knowing exactly where I was. When, finally, I came to my senses and was about to get up, I heard somebody screaming for help. I didn't stop to think: I got up, with some difficulty, and ran in the direction of the screams.

It was the clearing where Isabel and I had performed our play. And there was Sílvia. What she was doing there by herself, I had no idea. Had she come looking for the Indian on her own? What was clear is that she was immobilized, paralyzed by fear. And soon I discovered why. In front of her, curled around the tree, was the snake. Our snake. Neither Adamastor nor myself had taken the effort to remove it. After all, we weren't expecting visitors—much less an easily frightened visitor like, it seems, Sílvia.

My first impulse was to reassure her: don't be scared, it's not a real snake. But then I realized: I couldn't speak. Not in Portuguese at least. But I also couldn't leave, abandoning the poor girl there. What could I do? Quickly, I decided. I jumped into the clearing, went over to the tree, grabbed from it the snake, showed it to Sílvia without a word, threw it on the ground, and stepped on it.

Relieved, she laughed. And I was about to disappear again into the jungle when she, now stern, grabbed me by the arm.

"Wait. I know who you are."

She looked me in the eyes:

"You're an actor. I saw you in that play, *Hamlet in Brasília*. Ricardo is your name, if I recall correctly."

Can you believe it? Of all the inhabitants of Brazil, only a miniscule fraction had seen that play. And Sílvia Campos was one of those people. Wow, that was some serious dedication to the theater. And that was some really bad luck.

"You're a good actor," she went on, smiling. "I should say that, for me, you were the perfect Indian."

She wasn't upset, she wasn't shouting at the top of her lungs that I was a shameless con artist. No. She had unmasked me, that was more than obvious, but apparently she was dealing with this revelation calmly. This was a relief to me, but also intriguing. As if reading my mind, she explained.

"I have a certain familiarity with fraud. You see, my father was a famous con man. He sold stock in a company that didn't exist. Because of that, he had to go on the lam. He's lived in Africa for many years. Once in a while he writes. And Adamastor isn't the first one to come up with stories about helpless Indians. There was a rancher in Pará who requested a million dollars to help a tribe. It's just the tribe was made up of his wife's relatives."

"What are you going to do?" I asked.

"Good question, Ricardo. Good question. We have two alternatives."

That "we have" represented a considerable relief: she wasn't looking at me as an enemy, or at least not as an outright enemy.

"What are they?"

"The first: I tell Gunnar that you've put on a farce. Then it's up to him what to do. He might leave things be—we'll leave and nothing will happen. Or he can report you to the police, as he did with that rancher from Pará."

An entirely unpleasant prospect.

"And the other one?"

"The other you'll have to propose. How are you going to get out of this without pulling one over on the Swedes and without ruining your life or Adamastor's life? You decide. Use your imagination."

My imagination, unfortunately, wasn't helping. At that moment, at least. I desperately tried to come up with an answer to Sílvia's question, but nothing came to me.

"Give me some time," I asked.

"Twenty-four hours," she said. "That's what you have. Gunnar wants to leave at noon tomorrow. Before then, the problem will need to be resolved. If not, I'll tell him the truth."

She wasn't fooling around. She was a serious girl, Sílvia. Which only heightened the admiration I felt for her, even if her response had intimidated me. Noticing, she smiled.

"Don't worry, Ricardo. I know you're going to come up with a solution. You came up with the story of the Indian. Now come up with a way to make him go away."

She pointed at the serpent.

"But it will have to be something as convincing as that snake. It really had me scared."

She pulled me toward her and kissed me. On the mouth. Which surprised me. She, on the other hand, just laughed.

"It's just a way of saying thanks: after all, you saved me from a terrible fright."

And she left. I stayed there a few minutes, ecstatic—what had just happened? But then I realized that there was no time to lose. I ran to the hideout, grabbed the cell phone, and called Adamastor.

"I can't talk right now," he said. "I'll call you in a little while."

He must have been meeting with the Swede. I waited, in anguish. A few minutes later—centuries for me—he called. I told him what had happened, and he panicked.

"I knew this wouldn't work, I knew it! Now what? What are we going to do?"

I told him to calm down; after all, he couldn't let his agitation show.

"Calm down, Adamastor. We're going to get out of this, I guarantee. Let me think of something. I'll call you right back."

I sat down. I needed to come up with a way out. Work, stupid brain, work, I muttered. To no avail. I couldn't see a way to save the Indian. Our Peri was doomed. And his inventors too.

Peri.

Of course! Peri. Why hadn't I thought of that sooner?

At the end of *The Guarani*, Peri and the heroine, Ceci, are trapped by floodwaters. They climb up a palm tree. The Indian is able to pull the tree from the ground, and the two of them float away—and they disappear into the horizon. José de Alencar doesn't bother to tell us where they went, it wasn't necessary. What was important was that they disappear.

Now, making our Indian disappear would be easy. What would be hard would be to come up with a way for him to disappear that would be convincing to the Swede.

And then José de Alencar helped me again. Like Peri, I would disappear into the horizon—of the sea. That vast sea facing us. Only I wouldn't go by palm tree, of course. Nor by swimming. No. I would go by *piroga*, that dugout canoe used by Indians. Adamastor had one, in his garage. The old owner had left it there, telling him that it had belonged, in fact, to Indians.

I called Adamastor, we arranged for the final details of Operation Peri.

The next day, leaving the house, they would find old clothing in front of the door. Adamastor should demonstrate surprise, unpleasant surprise. He would explain that those were the gifts that he had given to the young Indian. It would appear that he was returning them. Then they would spot the canoe on the sea down below. With his binoculars, Gunnar and Sílvia would identify the Indian. He's leaving, Adamastor would say. And he would attribute this flight precisely to the presence of strangers.

13

AN ENDING THAT MIGHT EVEN BE CONSIDERED HAPPY

That's exactly what happened. The only problem was having to keep the rocking of the canoe under control. But my experience as a surfer helped, so soon I was excitedly paddling while, from the porch of the house, they watched me. Gunnar, Adamastor later told me, was distressed: after all, he had just wanted to help. And this was the result: the Indian was leaving.

"Where is he going?" he asked, anxiously. Adamastor reassured him.

"Don't worry, he'll soon find another place to live. There is still a lot of forest in this area."

"But he won't be on your land."

"No. Certainly not."

"A shame," said Sílvia, quite serious.

"Indeed. But, on the other hand, I'll be able to host more visitors interested in ecotourism. With the Indian here, it was a problem. A problem we no longer have."

I didn't go very far. As soon as I made it around the peninsula at the base of the mountain, I beached the canoe. I went to

103

the nearby town and found a barbershop. I went in. The barber looked me over from head to toe. Not without reason: I was still wearing that strange loincloth. I thought it best to introduce myself.

"I work with Adamastor."

His face broke out in a smile.

"The one from Eden-Brazil?"

"You know him?"

"Not personally. But I saw the guy on television."

He looked at me, inquisitively.

"As a matter of fact, I think I know you too. Your picture was in the paper. Weren't you Adam, in that play everyone was talking about?"

"I was."

"You were? You aren't anymore?"

I told him we had ended the project.

"That's a shame," he said. "You might have brought a lot of tourists to our region."

He sighed.

"Well, it's no use crying over spilt milk. What'll it be?"

I sat in the chair and asked him to cut off all my hair.

"But," I added, "I don't have any money on me. I went out only in this loincloth, you see."

He laughed.

"That's okay. You artists are just as absentminded as they say you are. Your credit is good with me. You really want me to cut it all off? Don't tell me you're going to join up with those guys, the . . ."

"Skinheads? No, my friend. It's just because of the heat."

From town I got a ride to a spot close to Adamastor's property. I went the rest of the way on foot. I entered the house through the back, went to my room, got dressed—suit and tie—put on some dark glasses, and looked at myself in the mirror. Perfect: nothing of Peri remained.

I went out again through the back and went to knock on the front door. Adamastor opened it.

"Ricardo! What a surprise! Come in, come in."

Gunnar and Sílvia were there—she was impassive.

"I want to introduce to you a friend, Ricardo. He's an actor. He took part in a play that we put on here at the property, but that is no longer being presented. Ricardo was traveling—and now he's back."

He winked at Sílvia.

"Wanting to spend the summer here for free, I presume. But you're always welcome, Ricardo. Let me introduce you to my visitors. This here is Mr. Gunnar, representative of a Swedish foundation, and this is Sílvia, his assistant. They came because of that Indian that was living here in the jungle, you remember?"

"I remember. And they're going to help the Indian?"

"They were going to. The guy took off, Ricardo. He took a canoe and he left, to who knows where."

"That's a shame. The last Indian in the region, he certainly added some value to your property . . ."

Before the Swede had a chance to wonder what I meant by that statement, Sílvia looked at the clock.

"We have to get going. It's almost noon; we can't miss our flight."

We said our goodbyes. Sílvia's hand paused in mine. Just a fraction of a second, but enough to convey the message: our complicity was confirmed. Our complicity and perhaps something else? There was no time to clear up the issue: the two were already heading out the door.

"I'm going to take them to the airport," said Adamastor. "We'll talk later, Ricardo."

There was no third play. Which left me wondering about one thing, or, better, left me wondering about two things. In the first place, what might the third play have been? *Peri in Eden?* Maybe. It wasn't a bad idea. Second, might it have worked? The third time's a charm: "The first was her father, the second her brother, and the third was to whom she gave her hand." She, the goddess Fortune. Or the goddess Love. Sílvia Campos? Yes, for some time she inhabited my fantasies, but the fact is I never saw her again. For the best, a voice in my head tells me: she was too perfect, too blond, too aristocratic. The argument didn't matter to me, but I did want to know whose voice that was. I suspect that it's my father's, speaking from some remote and strange indigenous heaven, a heaven where Guarani angels play flutes, like they did in the Jesuit missions.

I went back to Porto Alegre. My mother, in poor health, needed me; my sister, a flight attendant, couldn't abandon her schedule of flights. Little by little, mother forgave me. More than that, she got me a job: I teach theater in a private school run by a friend of hers. I don't make much, but enough to live on. And the kids are so funny. There's one who can recite poetry really well. Not Gonçalves Dias, but he does recite poetry—some verses he learned on TV.

I haven't stayed in touch with Adamastor, but I know he's not doing too badly in life. Eden-Brazil is now a regular hotel that receives tourists from São Paulo, from Rio Grande do Sul, and from Argentina. The person who sends them there, incredible as it seems, is Gutiérrez. After his business in Mexico failed and after breaking up with Isabel, who left him for a mariachi musician, he returned to Argentina, where, together with a friend, he started a travel agency. And he began to send entire tour groups to Eden-Brazil.

Of the place, I have fond memories. And two souvenirs: a stuffed monkey—poor Lucifer died, and Adamastor, I'm not sure why, gave the animal to me as a present—and the head of Maria Angélica, the serpent of Paradise. The voice chip still works perfectly, and sometimes I go to sleep listening to that voice, promising to reveal unknown marvels and pleasures. When that happens, I dream—about Peri and Ceci on the palm tree, floating on the turbulent waters. Ceci looks at him passionately. Peri, concerned, says something like: I hope this piece of shit doesn't sink. Ceci unexpectedly begins to sing. And then the sharp sounds of her voice turn into the sound of the alarm clock. Someday we'll have to wake up, don't you think?

TRANSLATOR'S NOTE

I first stumbled upon Moacyr Scliar's late novella, *Éden-Brasil*, as I browsed through a brief section of Brazilian literature in a Lisbon bookstore in the summer of 2008. It was, I felt at the time, precisely the book I had been looking for, something to fill out a corpus of contemporary Brazilian novels I'd been writing about that explore rural place and identity in a society and in a literature that in recent decades had become overwhelmingly urban. My encounter with the book seemed doubly fortuitous in that I hadn't noticed it in any bookstores I'd visited in Brazil over the years, nor was I later able to find any reviews or promotional press coverage from around the time of its original publication in 2002. It seemed almost apocryphal, though Scliar's extreme prolificacy (he authored more than seventy books during his lifetime, and in 2002 alone he published a total of four titles) and the novella's classification as young adult literature made it more reasonable to deduce that it simply had dropped under the radar and garnered no critical attention.

In any case, I was excited to have discovered Scliar's novel, but as I read and thought about it alongside works by Antônio Torres, Conceição Evaristo, Adriana Lisboa, and Ronaldo Correia de Brito, among others, it soon revealed itself to be something of an outlier, orbiting some common themes and questions, but rather distantly and distinctly. All of the novels I had gathered feature protagonists returning, physically or through memory, from cities to which they had migrated back to their lost rural origins, in ways that both evoked and also skeptically interrogated pastoral idealizations of country life. However, Scliar's skepticism and his lighthearted gestures toward satire in *Éden-Brasil*, and even the undertones of melancholy, seemed differently directed. In short, among this grouping of what I came to describe as postregionalist, counterpastoral novels, Scliar's work, intriguingly, set itself apart as more of a playful reflection on environmentalism and the environmental imagination in and of Brazil as deeply structured by myths of paradise and paradise lost and Romantic depictions of nature and native peoples.

After concluding that essay on rural place and identity in Brazilian narrative, and even after adjusting the focus of my scholarship to environmental engagement and ecological thinking in the work of Brazilian poets and visual artists, Scliar's novel continued to intrigue me. More precisely, I imagined that the novel, if translated into English, might find its way into conversations and curricula emerging from the developing fields of ecocriticism and environmental humanities, at a moment when they were struggling to become less parochial and more global or transnational, extending canonical horizons beyond Anglo-American nature writing. Adding a perspective from the Global South, Scliar's novel illustrates broadly salient questions about the ethics, politics, and practical impacts of conservation, development, and ecotourism, as well as more historically and culturally contingent visions of the relationship between nature, indigeneity, and national identities. Moreover, for Anglophone readers looking for insight into Brazil through contemporary literature, *Eden-Brazil* lightly evokes, in an engaging and accessible manner, key aspects of the culture, society, and history of Brazil often addressed in introductory Portuguese and Brazilian studies courses here in the United States. It touches on racism and racial identities, corruption, the *jeitinho*, and the popular *malandro* trickster archetype, land reform and the Landless Movement, the period of the military dictatorship and its aftermaths, and regional diversity in Brazil. Its repeated references to the "Indianist" novels of the nineteenth-century writer José de Alencar present an opportunity to consider the enduring legacies of Romantic representations of native Brazilians and of tropical nature. And the novel's invoking of the stories of Genesis recalls the Edenic myths and motifs that have informed the imaginary of Brazil, and the New World at large, back to the earliest periods of discovery and colonization. With these imagined readers in mind, I decided to attempt a translation of the novel.

The actual translation of the novel was a rather straightforward endeavor. Scliar's crisply direct storytelling mode is sustained throughout the novel, and his language, though evoking a conversational informality and thus eschewing rarefied terms or lyrical turns, is standard Brazilian Portuguese and not at all regionally inflected. Even his Argentine *malandro* character, the roguish Ernesto Gutiérrez, is provided an unaccented Portuguese in his moments of dialogue. And while the environment is thematically central and the story is precisely set in the coastal Santa Catarina state, where impressive remains of the Mata Atlântica, the Atlantic Forest, cover mountains as they dramatically drop to meet the sea, there is very little descriptive specificity as relates to the region's socio-biodiversity, which might have presented

particular challenges for translation. Ironically, the one significant listing in the novel of what would be for Anglophone readers
exotic animal species are also exotic to the novel's setting itself,
as Adamastor reviews an inventory of options to try to populate
his forest turned theme park with charismatic fauna. What did
require more care and attention was the effort to faithfully convey in translation the novel's narrative voice and its varied tones,
as it shifted back and forth between matter-of-factness, slight
sarcasm and perhaps even mocking cynicism, idealism, compas-
sion, and wistfulness. What aided me here was some growing
familiarity with this narrative voice—even as it's attributed to the
young, aspiring actor Richie—as typically Scliar-like. Though I
had read a handful of Scliar's other, better known novels over the
years, around the time I decided to try translating *Éden-Brasil*, in
another fortuitous coincidence, I also began to read, together with
students, a collection of his *crônicas*, or essays, gathered together
in an intermediate Portuguese language reader.* These readings,
covering a wide range of topics, from a search for Emily Dickin-
son's gravestone during a visit to Amherst, Massachusetts, to an
epic Cold War–inflected struggle for space with a Russian man
on a Prague streetcar, gave me a more firmly established sense
of Scliar's voice, his sense of humor, his penchant for the absurd,
his intense yet nondoctrinaire interest in politics and religion,
his gleefully mocking yet still deeply compassionate attention to
human foibles (including his own), and his unwavering commit-
ment to the value of a good story and the craft of storytelling.
The other challenge I grappled with in Scliar's prose is his ten-
dency toward extremely long sentences that resist the same sense
of flow in a straightforward English translation. These sentences

---

* *Viajando através do alfabeto*, edited by Patrícia Isabel Sobral and Clemence
Jouët-Pastré and published in 2009.

are often unusually punctuated, with a quite liberal use of parentheses, colons, and semicolons. While I made a good faith effort to retain his particular style for crafting his sentences, I confess that there is some domestication in this translation in this regard, a decision that was confirmed and encouraged by editors.

I regret that I didn't have the chance to discuss or exchange any correspondence with Moacyr Scliar about my efforts to translate this novel. He died in early 2011, before I had fully committed to undertaking the project (the first draft of the translation I completed only in 2014). I would be curious to know not only his thoughts on the translation, but his opinions on the novel itself and how it holds up at the present moment, given the intensification of environmental battles present and looming, and the renewed visibility of indigenous peoples' struggles for territorial and human rights, in Brazil and globally. Would he have second thoughts about the rather ambiguous way in which these questions are treated in his story, oscillating somewhere between heartfelt engagement and ironic distance? I rather suspect that he would be too busy writing new stories to have second thoughts, and that he would trust us, his readers, to grapple with the ambiguities, to draw inspiration from them for discussion, disagreement, debate, and, even our own rewritings of his environmentalist parable.

With that desire to inspire reflection on environmentalism and environmental justice in mind, I'd like to express my gratitude to Tagus Press and its editorial team, especially Mario Pereira, Dário Borim, and Cristina Mehrtens, for their support for the publication of this translation and for their careful attention to the manuscript. I'd also like to acknowledge the support of my friend and colleague, Marguerite Itamar Harrison, an accomplished translator herself and a treasured interlocutor on Brazilian literature, art, culture, and politics. I'd also like to thank

Rex Nielson and Odile Cisneros, both of whom were inspiring colleagues as we together attempted to bring environmental criticism into the field of Brazilian literary and cultural studies. Of course, I'm ever grateful to my partner, Erotides Sturião Silva, fellow traveler through the world and through the many worlds of shared readings and stories. And, finally, I'm grateful to my students of Portuguese and Brazilian studies at Smith College, for their enthusiasm, idealism, intelligence, and instincts for caring and justice. This translation is dedicated to them and to those to come.

Malcolm K. McNee